THE
FOOLS'
WAR

THE FOOLS' WAR

by Lee Kisling

HarperCollins*Publishers*

Library of Congress Cataloging-in-Publication Data
Kisling, Lee R.
  The fools' war / by Lee Kisling.
    p.   cm.
  Summary: A boy must try to save a kingdom when the king, preoccupied by unrequited
love, ignores the threat of war.
  ISBN 0-06-020836-8. — ISBN 0-06-020837-6 (lib. bdg.)
  [1. Kings, queens, rulers, etc.—Fiction.   2. War—Fiction.]   I. Title.
PZ7.K6665Fo   1992   91-47695
[Fic]—dc20   CIP
                                                                           AC

1   2   3   4   5   6   7   8   9   10
First Edition

A Court with no Queen, a shepherd, a soldier
A fool with a spoon and a ring
A wart in the eye of the beholder as fine
As the jewel in the crown of a King.

Contents

THE
FOOLS'
WAR

A Soul With One Shoe

White-haired old Fedde took a final blurred view of his wife, Jude, and his kind-faced youngest son, Clemmy, who were talking quietly at his bedside. He watched their lips move. He saw their heads nodding in agreement and occasionally turning to look at him. And then he closed his eyes for the last time, heard their voices fade. It was a gentle passage into regions beyond life that no one has ever charted. Clemmy, the son, barely fifteen years old, pulled a sheepskin blanket up to his father's chin, stroked his thin white hair, and silently said good-bye. Mother and son embraced tearfully. Outside in the morning air a young goat kicked up his heels.

For the sake of setting the scene, it is perhaps useful to imagine Fedde's soul as it slips away from his body, away from the goat pens and garden, soaring into the fresh morning air above the thatch-roofed cottage, circling higher and higher and looking down on the green pastures and forests. From that height we can survey the hills and valleys, the big river and the simple homes along its banks. We can see two monks moving along a forest path—one riding a pony and frowning, and one walking behind and fanning the air with a piece of birchbark.

Winging north, farther north than Fedde had ever been when he was alive, the departing soul would whistle over tall pines, over a great castle wall. Turning back to the south, it would cross the path of a huge army of warriors wearing turbans, galloping on black horses and waving their terrible blades.

If the soaring could make a vapor trail as the modern jets do, and if it could read and write, which old Fedde had never learned to do, it might have written GOOD-BYE AND GOOD LUCK! Or, more likely, it would have circled back to paint the sky over his cottage, Clemmy's cottage now, with the words: BE CAREFUL, BOY. BE CAREFUL.

Clemmy buried his father under pine trees that same day, working quietly with his spade. The grave was marked with smooth red and gray river stones and was decorated with a bouquet of wildflowers Jude had gathered and tucked tenderly among the stones. She sat nearby then and rocked side to side, humming an old tune.

By the standard of the times, Fedde and Jude

were prosperous. They raised their own food and animals and traded their surplus in a village two miles distant. Fedde had not been to the village for over a year because his legs had become feeble, so the trading and most of the homestead work had been taken over by Clemmy. Weekly trips to the market were made by mother and son until Jude developed the neurotic (and dangerous) habit of stealing things at the marketplace. The old woman was becoming feebleminded with age, and Clemmy, who at first was amused, finally decided to leave his old mom home for her own safety.

Even there, sitting together under the pines, Clemmy knew that Jude, her cheeky old face wrapped in a homespun scarf, had hidden in the pocket of her woolen robe one of Fedde's shoes, a shoe pilfered from a corpse about to be buried. It was funny, Clemmy thought; and carrying his dad to the pine grove missing a shoe, followed by his mother, Clemmy wept tears of love and loss for them both. Wherever Fedde's soul is headed, shoes probably don't matter, he thought. He sat and listened to Jude humming the old song. After a while she rested her head on his shoulder and Clemmy held her.

"He was a good old dad," he said quietly.

"Yes."

"They are pretty flowers you picked."

"Flowers. Yes."

"He liked flowers."

"Me too." A light afternoon breeze stirred the pines softly, and a bird sang above them.

"He won't get far, Clemmy, because I've got his shoe," she said matter-of-factly.

"I know you do."

sympathy from Garth.

"I fetch the coins, so I ride the horse," Garth said. "When you put a single penny in the box, then you can ride and I'll walk. Ha!"

Hans knew that meant he would be walking a long time.

The black-and-white pony's gastronomic troubles had to do only partly with turnips. The pressure placed on all his internal organs by his oversized load was certainly no aid to digestion. He plodded slowly forward. After many miles he sniffed the smoke of the village fires and breathed a short whinny of relief. Brother Garth's sandals dug into the pony's flanks, and the animal plodded on.

When they reached the village, Brother Garth moved among the people in his great wide robe, offering blessings on the eggs and woolen cloth. He smiled widely and rattled the poor box. When charity failed to withdraw the peasants' funds, Garth resorted to commerce, holding aloft the letters of indulgence. No one in the village was particularly glad to see him. And then, luckily for Brother Garth, Clemmy arrived.

He had come from the opposite direction, carrying a basket of brown eggs. In the village market he told the sad news of his father's death. The large monk made the sign of the cross, spoke some words Clemmy didn't understand, and invited himself (and Hans) to Clemmy's homestead for the night. They would say proper prayers over Fedde's grave.

When they reached his small cottage, Clemmy awakened Jude, who was snoozing in their best wicker chair. She set places at the table for Garth, whom she knew, and for Hans, whom she had never seen. Supper would be simple—boiled eggs and bread and butter. Garth said a prayer at the table. When they had finished eating, Clemmy and Brother Hans went outside to do evening chores. They carried water from the stream, milked the fresh nanny goats and turned their bedding grass. They gathered eggs and pulled weeds from the wide garden beside the house. The monks' pony grazed among the goats and drank from their water barrel. Twilight overtook them at last, and they went back inside.

Garth was snoring peacefully on Clemmy's straw mattress, and Jude was slumped in her chair, sound asleep. Clemmy carried his mother to her bed and covered her with soft hides. She seemed light as a feather and did not wake up. He gathered several more blankets and led Brother Hans outside again.

Clemmy was tall for a boy of fifteen. He had a boyish mop of brown hair and pale-green eyes. He was solidly built from hard work on the farm and had a quietness about him and a pleasing smile. When Clemmy had been born, his older brothers and sisters were already grown. They had all sailed away downriver by the time he was six years old. He could scarcely remember them.

In the failing twilight Hans and Clemmy gathered kindling and threw sparks from a flint to start a fire. Wrapped in blankets and sitting on goat hides, they watched the smoke from their small fire curl upward. A star appeared.

"You have a fine homestead," Hans said.

"Yes. It is lonely, though, sometimes. There are only two of us now." Clemmy sighed. He threw a few more sticks into the fire and pulled his blanket around his shoulders to keep off the chill.

"I was wondering something, Brother Hans," Clemmy said.

"Hmmm?" Hans yawned. He was tired from all the walking.

"I was wondering about the money in the poor box. Does it really go to the poor?"

"Well, Clemmy, I don't honestly know. I suppose some of it does. Some of it goes to support the monastery and some of it goes to fight the Turk," Hans said.

Clemmy shivered at the idea of the Turk. Some people in the village said the Turks were marching a great army in their direction, but Clemmy didn't believe them. They said it every year in the springtime. Brother Hans spoke again.

"In a way, it really doesn't matter where the money goes, I think."

"What do you mean?"

"It comforts people to give coins to the church.

It's a sacrifice they make to believe in something, to believe in charity and love, and judgment, too."

"Garth frightens them with judgment and hell. It's not very comforting," Clemmy objected.

"But surely there's a hell, Clemmy. Can you imagine how people would behave if they didn't believe in hell? And they'll get along without their few pennies, won't they?"

People don't behave very well anyway, Clemmy thought, smiling into the darkness.

"Tomorrow Brother Garth will want to sell us one of your papers," he said. "And then my father gets into heaven, is that right?"

"Pope Leo's letter of forgiveness, yes," Hans answered. "'As soon as the coin in the coffer rings, the soul from purgatory springs!' That's what Garth says. And do you have a coin, Clemmy, to put in Garth's poor box?"

"I do. I have two coins," Clemmy answered. "I want forgiveness for my mother, too."

"Well, all right. Two letters! I'm sure Garth would agree to it." And then Brother Hans got an idea.

"Clemmy, would you mind giving me the coins instead of giving them to Garth? I'll put them in the box before he wakes up." He smiled at the pile of orange coals, remembering Garth's oath to let him ride the pony if he, Hans, put a single coin in the poor box.

The Paradise of Delight

The light of the first dawn put a glow on the horizon, and a cock's crow stirred Clemmy from sleep. The stars were fading overhead and the air was still. He rose and stretched his arms over his head and shook the sleep away from him. He nudged Brother Hans awake and they spoke softly.

The bargain they had struck the night before was now carried out. Without awakening Jude or Brother Garth, they slipped inside the house. Clemmy got his coins and Hans his saddlebags. Outside again, Hans produced the letters of indulgence from Pope Leo. The stiff yellow paper crackled as he unrolled it and Clemmy saw Brother Hans' neat penmanship. It was, Clemmy thought, the prettiest manmade thing he had ever seen.

Brother Hans pulled from his bag a small ink bottle. He removed the cork and dipped a quill pen. Near the top of the paper, just below the cross, he wrote the word *Fedde,* and on a second letter he wrote the word *Jude.*

"That's how you write your parents' names," Hans told Clemmy, indicating which was which. Clemmy took the letters in his hands, marveling at Hans' skill. He reached out his arm and gave the monk his coins without ever taking his eyes off the paper.

Later on, after chores and breakfast, the four hiked the short distance to Fedde's grave and Garth spoke prayers, but with little enthusiasm. He was clearly annoyed at Brother Hans for getting the coins. That was *his* job.

Clemmy, himself, had no second thoughts about giving up the money. He had the letters! He wondered at the miraculous power of these written words. He wanted to hear them spoken.

He got his wish after the prayers beside the grave. Hans recited the letter from memory, for he had written the words hundreds of times. Clemmy held Jude's small hand and listened to Hans intone the odd Latin syllables. When Hans had finished, he translated into their own language these phrases:

. . . *so that when you die, the gates of punishment shall be shut, and the gates of the paradise of delight shall be opened. And if you shall not die at present, this grace shall remain in full force when you are at the point of death.*

Clemmy and his mother bid farewell to the monks. Brother Garth insisted they accept a gift of turnips, and the two men were soon out of sight. Jude returned to her garden and sat quietly among the plants. The homestead work went on as before.

In the weeks that followed, Jude withdrew into her own private thoughts more and more. She spoke little and took no real interest in the letters of indulgence, which Clemmy often unrolled on their small table. She sat in the large chair, her eyes fixed on nothing, and she began to remember.

She remembered with great clarity her girlhood, her growing up, her affection for the shy young man Fedde who chased her one day and caught her around the waist, laughing. He tickled her and wrestled her down in high meadow grass. She remembered the laughing and the touching, the smell of the grass and the blue of the sky. Clemmy watched her giggle, close her eyes and blush. In these moments she was completely insensible to her actual surroundings—her son and his Latin letters—or to her stooped shoulders, wrinkles and gray hair. Watching her, Clemmy felt he was eavesdropping on the past.

Perhaps because he was so young and his memories were not as satisfying as his mother's, Clemmy was impatient to move forward. He drummed his fingers on the paper and looked about the room. It was all so familiar: the clothes hanging from pegs, the cooking pot, the butchering knife. He looked at the hides on their beds, the wild herbs hanging to dry. And then something unfamiliar on the mantelpiece caught his eye, something small and brown and rectangular. He walked quietly to the fireplace and picked it up.

Clemmy knew instantly what it was and also how it came to be there. It was Brother Hans' leatherbound, handwritten Bible. Although he couldn't read a word of it, he recognized the Latin letters and Hans' neat penmanship from the wonderful papers he had looked at over and over again. And he guessed that the book had been pilfered by his mother. At first he was surprised and even a little bit angry—stealing from a monk! But he remembered that all of Jude's sins were forgiven by the letter of indulgence. And anyway, it was an act of old-age foolishness, not as bad as some kinds of stealing.

It was also, Clemmy thought, an opportunity. He must return the book to Brother Hans.

Buying Marbelard

The next morning, after doing chores and settling Jude into her big chair with a cup of tea, Clemmy left the cottage and set out for the village.

The homes in the village were made of rough-hewn lumber, with thatched roofs, front gardens and animal sheds. They were built on a high bank that overlooked a river and were surrounded by forests. In a broad open area in the village center, there were butchering tables and water barrels, carts with firewood and animal skins. As more and more metal tools became available, tradesmen settled in the village. There were weavers and leather workers in addition to the herdsmen and farmers and fishermen. One day each week the village people traded their goods, gossiped and argued. There were occasional wrestling matches with no rules whatever. A ring of bystanders would make bets and then cheer or hoot loudly. On market day young people teased and flirted together and chickens ran about wildly. Un-washed children played games of chase, stirring up the flies and the dust.

Clemmy made for the weaver's cottage. His plan was to ask the village weaver to allow one of his sons to stay on the farm for a few days and look after Jude, while he made his way to the monastery and Brother Hans. For this he would exchange milk and eggs.

It was still early and no one was about. Suddenly the door of a ramshackle cottage burst open and a hunchbacked figure in tattered clothing hobbled quickly toward the gate. Clemmy heard an angry voice calling out, and a large man appeared in the doorway. It was Stotts, a fisherman who was almost always drunk on ale. He had a short leather whip that he brought down on the hunchback's shoulder again and again.

"Fool of a son!" he roared. "Clumsy and good for nothing!"

Clemmy recognized the beaten young man to be Marbelard, the village idiot. His head leaned to one side, toward his hump, and his tongue stuck out. He had one withered hand. With his good hand he fumbled at the gate latch. He cried out in fear and his eyes were filled with tears. Marbelard's two eyes looked in different directions always. He stumbled through the gate. Stotts pushed him to the ground and went on beating him with the whip. Marbelard raised his one good arm to ward off blows.

"Fool!"

"No!"

"Idiot!"

"Noooo!"

"Clumsy birdbrain!" The whip came down with each charge.

"Stop!" Clemmy spoke in a loud voice. It seemed Stotts would beat helpless Marbelard with the whip until he bled. The man ignored Clemmy and raised his arm again.

"Stop it, man!" The fisherman turned abruptly toward Clemmy. He had a wasted appearance—bags under dark eyes and pale flabby skin. He was, in fact, diseased from drinking and no longer master of his own sad life. He opened and closed his eyes several times, blinking Clemmy into focus.

"Go away, farmer," he said.

"Will the boy be smarter or less clumsy after you've beaten him?" Clemmy asked.

"Mind your own business," Stotts barked. "He belongs to me and I'll beat him when it pleases me."

"But he helps you. You need him."

"Drank my ale and broke the flask!" Stotts turned his rage again toward Marbelard. He kicked him in the side.

"Didn't do it! You drank it yourself!" the hunchback cried. Stotts cursed him and brought his whip down again.

"I'll buy him from you!" Clemmy blurted out.

"What?"

"I said I'll buy him. Marbelard. Your son."

"You can't buy people," Stotts told Clemmy. Marbelard began crawling away, whimpering. His clothes were so dirty already that he seemed to blend in with the footpath.

"If I gave you a thousand gold pieces, would you sell him to me?"

Stotts threw his head back and laughed. His mood could apparently change very quickly. He said, "For a thousand gold pieces I'll put a ribbon in his hair! And you can have his dunce cap too," he sneered.

"He is for sale then, am I right?" Clemmy insisted.

"By Christ, he's a bargain at any price," Stotts cackled.

"I'll give you twenty chickens for him," Clemmy said quickly. "They are the best chickens anywhere, and they lay big brown eggs, but you can't beat them with a whip. Trade the eggs for a little grain to feed them."

Stotts rubbed his chin with one hand, considering the offer. Marbelard struggled to his feet and gave Clemmy a cautious glance. Under the circumstances, twenty laying hens for Marbelard was probably a trade in Stotts' favor. Though his mind was eroded from a lifetime of liquor, Stotts saw his advantage.

"Twenty chickens and a bag of grain," he bargained.

"Done," Clemmy answered, realizing then that his plan to find Brother Hans would have to be postponed. He and Marbelard eyed each other. The village fool's eyes had the appearance of looking at both Clemmy and Stotts at the same time. A childish happiness crossed the boy's face briefly, like a momentary sunbreak in the clouds. Clemmy approached him and gently brushed the dirt from his old brown robe. Marbelard flinched.

"Can you walk far?" Clemmy asked him softly.

"Walk? Yes, I walk, sir. And I catch fish, sir."

Marbelard's speech was slow and his tilted head bowed frequently. He was no longer a boy but less than a man. His filthy feet were bare, the left turned out to the side, and his withered hand he held pressed to his stomach. His face was not ugly to look at, though his tongue often went to the corner of his mouth. Marbelard's hair was cut ragged and short, probably with a fish knife, and standing still he was in constant motion, bobbing and weaving in place. As if to illustrate his answer, the idiot straightened and walked ten lopsided paces, turned and walked back to Clemmy. His face shifted into a hopeful smile, which was swept away by the sound of Stotts retching over his garden gate. The sight of the man was so disgusting that Clemmy had to look away.

"Do you have anything you want to bring with

you?" Clemmy asked.

"I got the crown jewels," Marbelard whispered, looking cautiously at his sick father. He dug deep into the pocket of his robe and held up a copper penny in his good hand.

"Nothing else to bring?"

"I got nothin' else."

Stotts had puked on his own fishy-smelling pant-legs. He turned back to Clemmy. "Two fools! Hah! But which one is the bigger fool, eh?" He pointed at his own son and then at Clemmy. "Take him, and bring me twenty fat chickens!"

A Dance With the King

Making their way home along the footpath, Clemmy and Marbelard walked slowly, Marbelard swaying and bobbing with his lopsided gait.

Clemmy had seen Marbelard many times in the village. He was cheerful usually, being too foolish to know how bad off he was. Marbelard's mother had run away from Stotts years ago. The man blamed his deformed son for her leaving, as a way of excusing his own cruelty, which had rained many blows on her as well. It was a fishy bit of logic for Stotts: He blamed the mother for the idiot son and the son for the absent wife.

Marbelard was eight years old when his mother ran away. After she had been gone a few days, Stotts lied to the boy, saying she was gone visiting. Then a week and a month brought other lies, until finally Marbelard's limited brain power figured out that she was gone forever, like a pretty rock that has been thrown in a pond. Whatever suffering the child's deformity brought him, nothing hurt so much as his loneliness. His eyes poured tears down from a great height, the highest branches of a beech tree at the river's edge. The villagers marveled at his agility in climbing the tree, persuading him, finally, to climb down. Kinder folk worked at cheering him up.

Over time his spirits improved. Clemmy saw him every market day helping Stotts carry fish and fish oil in pottery jugs to trade. Stotts never wasted any money getting clothing for Marbelard. The boy worked and didn't complain. As if nature had spent its reproach on his appearance, the boy was blessed with good health and a happy outlook. As for his wits, it was generally assumed that he was an idiot or a half-wit at best. He was not included in adult conversations. These conversations, it might be pointed out, were not exactly erudite philosophical debates, either.

"How do you feel?" Clemmy asked Marbelard when they stopped to rest.

"Strong enough to fight the Turk!" Marbelard answered oddly.

"We probably won't meet the Turk on this path," Clemmy laughed. "Have you ever been away from the village?"

"I've been to Vienna, sir, and danced with the King," Marbelard said seriously. It was such a laughable picture that Clemmy shook his head in amazement. He was also picturing his own affairs growing more complex, having become the young master of a farm with a mixed-up old woman and a grown-up idiot.

At last they made their way across the meadow to the cottage, where a wisp of smoke curled up from the chimney. Clemmy stopped and pointed.

"That's your new home. Do you see it?"

"Is my mother there?" Marbelard asked slowly.

"No. But my mother is there, and you can share her with me."

"Is she pretty?"

"Yes! She's very pretty." Clemmy laughed.

Jude was in the garden when they entered the small yard. Clemmy worked the gate latch as Marbelard swayed in the breeze behind him. They walked down the narrow garden path where the old woman was weeding a patch of new beans. She stood as they approached.

"You've brought Marbelard from the village," she said, wiping the dirt from her apron. Marbelard smiled broadly at hearing his name spoken. "He needs a bath, Clemmy."

Marbelard edged alongside Clemmy and bowed to Jude.

"This is Jude, my mother," Clemmy said.

"I know. I used to see her sometimes in the village," Marbelard stammered.

"He smells like fish!" Jude said.

"He's going to live here, with us." Clemmy gestured back toward the cottage.

"I've been bought and sold!" Marbelard said happily, looking at both Clemmy and Jude at the same time with his two-direction eyes.

"Does he lay eggs or give milk?" the old woman asked with a wry, wrinkled smile.

"I do!" Marbelard announced.

"He doesn't," Clemmy said.

"Well, he needs a bath anyway," Jude said.

Clemmy went off to draw buckets of water and to stoke the fire in the cottage. From inside the garden he heard more laughter as Jude and Marbelard pulled weeds.

In the days that followed, Marbelard helped with the chores; he learned how to milk a goat and turn a warm cloth placed over a clutch of eggs in a basket beside the fireplace. Clemmy had delivered his chickens to Stotts and was taking care to hatch a new brood.

Clemmy, of course, was watching to see if he could safely leave the homestead for a few days, to return the Bible to Brother Hans. Marbelard accomplished every task that was set for him and relished every kindness offered him. He seemed very proud of his new clothes and studied his reflection in the still pool of water that Clemmy had created by damming the stream near the house. He carried water and gathered wood, and he watched Jude constantly.

One day Marbelard announced, "There's a handsome prince in your pond."

"Oh, is there? And you've seen him?"

"Yes, I've seen him smiling."

"And is he very handsome?"

"Yes, and he's riding a white horse!" Marbelard fibbed. Clemmy and Jude laughed with pleasure.

"Marbelard," Clemmy addressed him warmly but with a serious tone.

"Yes, sir?"

"I need to go away for several days," Clemmy said. "Can you help getting the wood and fetching the water?"

"I can, sir!"

"And can you look after my mother and help with the milking?"

"I can do it!" Marbelard nodded vigorously. Old Jude smiled widely and gave Clemmy a wink, as if to say: Don't worry about us.

And so the next morning, with a bag of cheese and bread to eat and the Latin Bible in his pocket, he said good-bye. Across the meadow he turned and looked back to see Marbelard bobbing with pleasure and Jude brushing his hair.

Learning to Read

Everyone in the village knew where the monks' monastery could be found. Clemmy listened to a dozen different opinions and saw helpful fingers point every direction. No one, as it turned out, had ever actually been there but there was a consensus that north was the way to go. Clemmy left them to their arguing and took the up-river trail.

It was a fair spring day. He met no one on the path until late afternoon, when he overtook a traveling merchant who was resting himself and two donkeys. The donkeys were laden with trade goods. One was almost completely covered with cooking pots. The man was named Balfounder, and he was talkative and glad for some company.

"The monastery? You would be referring to St. Euchre, with the well-fed Brother Garth? Yes, I know where it is, but my own path leads to Mulberia, farther north."

"What is Mulberia?" Clemmy wanted to know.

"You've never heard of King Fernholz the Lame, of Mulberia?"

"Never. Is he a wise king?"

"Welllllll, some say he is. Some say not. He does say wise sayings, all right, but I've heard better round about. I suppose he's a good enough king. People like him." Balfounder chewed on a twig. He sat on the ground with his back against a tree. He wore a fine robe and excellent boots.

"Can you tell me any of his wise sayings?" Clemmy asked with interest.

"Welllllll, let me think. . . . Oh yes, I remember. Fernholz the Lame said: 'Don't paint in your good pants.'"

"That seems wise," Clemmy said.

"Not bad, not bad. He also said: 'A king with no sons is like a pond with no fish.' But he didn't like that so well, so he changed it to: 'A king with no sons is like a cart with no wheels.'"

"Hmmmmm."

"Yes, you're right. It lacks something. Maybe he'll change it again." Balfounder tossed away his chewing twig.

"Has he no sons?" Clemmy asked.

"No queen! Though many would marry him. But there will soon be a wedding, for the King has fallen in love. Lost his mind with love." The trader winked at Clemmy. "It's good for business. I sell him pretty things and he gives them to the lady as gifts. Pieces of silk and lace, and rugs and coffee, which I buy from the Turk. In fact, that's where I got these things," Balfounder said, pointing at the goods on his donkeys.

Clemmy was shocked. The Turk! Never having seen one, he half-believed the Turk was imaginary.

"You've talked to the Turk?" he asked.

"Oh yes. I've sat in their tents! They are a cut-throat bunch, I'll tell you, but they're not above a little commerce now and then, though they would rather murder and steal."

"Forgive me, Balfounder, but why don't they kill you?"

"Turk's funny that way," the man answered. "As for me, I care nothing about the faith, you see, nothing. Nor do I care about priests or kings or sultans and their wars. And I don't care who hates who and who loves who. I'm a businessman, you see? It's all the same to me.

"You may as well ask: How many gods are there? Is there a separate god for Christians and the Turk? What I have to say is: Who cares? The Turk prays for victory and the Pope prays for salvation and the Jew prays not to get caught between them! It's a funny world, you see, and the sky is full of prayers. I would guess there must be a thousand gods just to handle the prayer end of things. And a hundred more to handle the weather and the stars."

It began to sound to Clemmy like a business enterprise.

"You must have traveled far," he said, to change the subject.

"Welllllll, it gets shorter every year. The Turk's on the move again and coming this way, bound for Vienna, if he can find it. He has poor map-reading skills. The Turk may hack you to pieces, son, but he will probably ask for directions first."

They walked together several miles until Balfounder turned west with his donkeys. He pointed north and east and bid Clemmy fair journey.

"It's many miles. Where the river turns east, leave it and walk toward those hills. You should be there before sundown tomorrow."

Clemmy slept in a forest clearing under a million stars. In the morning he followed Balfounder's directions and came upon a well-traveled path that led him to the monastery.

The monks' home was the largest building Clemmy had ever seen, tucked into a valley between the high hills. It had a bell tower with a wooden cross on top. The building was made of stone with a tiled roof and great stone chimneys. There was a large garden on two sides surrounded by a tumble-down stone wall.

Suddenly bells began to peal from the monastery tower and Clemmy heard men's low voices singing. It was a rather slow and uninteresting song, Clemmy thought, and the men sang out of tune and not quite together. He strained to hear the Latin words as he made his way down the hillside path and crossed over a decaying footbridge that spanned a small creek.

The heavy monastery door was closed. Clemmy was just about to have a pull on the door when it jerked and creaked open before him, sagging on one broken hinge. Clemmy stepped back and found himself suddenly face-to-face with Brother Garth, who filled the doorway with his huge robe.

"Hellooooo Clemmy," Garth said, with exaggerated friendliness. "You've come a long way from home. Anything wrong? Old mom pass away?"

"No no. She's fine, thank you, Brother Garth. I've just—"

"Someone die in the village?" Garth interrupted.

"Uh, not that I know of. I'm just—"

"Someone mortally ill and wanting last rites?"

"Well, no, I don't think so. I was just—"

"What do you want, then? Why have you come here?" Garth asked irritably.

"To see Brother Hans!" Clemmy said quickly.

"To see Brother Hans? What on earth for?"

"He left something. A book. I'm returning it."

Brother Garth rolled his eyes and sighed. "Oh, I see. Well, you'll find him reciting Psalms in the carrot patch, probably." Garth pointed toward the garden and tramped away down the path without a good-bye. Clemmy heard the planks on the foot-bridge creak under the large monk.

Clemmy walked into the wide monastery garden, and, as Garth had predicted, spotted Brother Hans nearby, arms outstretched, speaking Latin to all plants within earshot. Clemmy smiled and thought of Marbelard. Maybe Marbelard would talk to his beans and cabbages. He stood still and listened to Hans' soothing voice: *"Auribus percipe verba oris me."*

Having said this (whatever it was) to the greens all around him, Brother Hans went to work with his hoe, jabbing at weeds. Clemmy approached him on the garden path and at last called out, "Hello, Brother Hans." The monk turned and waved in recognition.

"Clemmy! My, what a long way you've come! I'm so glad to see you. But why?"

"To return your book," Clemmy said, withdrawing the small Bible from his side pocket. "It was . . . left at my cottage," he said shyly, avoiding Brother Hans' gaze lest the monk guess the rest.

Brother Hans' eyes widened at the sight of it. He took the book in his hands and held it to his heart.

"Thank you," he said, shaking Clemmy's hand warmly. "Thank you very much, Clemmy. I suppose I must have dropped it. Are you hungry?"

Leaving the plants to visit among themselves, they walked out of the garden and into the monastery kitchen. Brother Hans cut some bread and served a bowl of thin soup to his guest. Clemmy wondered how Brother Garth could maintain his size on this meager food.

"Will you stay the night, Clemmy?"

"Yes thank you, but I must start out early tomorrow," Clemmy answered. He drained his bowl and set it down slowly.

"Brother Hans . . ."

"Yes?"

"Will you teach me to read?" He said it quickly, as if to get it off his chest. He had been thinking this thought ever since he first saw the beautiful letters of indulgence. It was an odd thing to want, he knew. Nobody in the village could read or write. There was no ink and no paper and no books.

Brother Hans fanned the pages of his little book. Looking very pleased, he said, "Of course I will teach you."

"I only have a penny to pay you." It was Marbelard's coin.

"It's more than enough," Brother Hans answered.

And so the reading lesson began. Hans and Clemmy retired to Hans' private room, which had a window, a narrow bed and a small table. Hans started by teaching Clemmy the Latin alphabet. They recited the letters (twenty-four in all) over and over until the pupil could do it by himself. Next came the phonetic sounding out of simple words and phrases, repeated again and again.

After more hard bread and gruel, the Latin lesson went on by lamplight in Brother Hans' tiny room until the monk fell asleep. Clemmy watched the stars through the small window, and he heard owls calling to one another from high on the hillside. Finally he lay on his blanket and dreamed about being the wise king and marrying a fine lady.

When he woke up, he found Brother Hans already at the table, writing with a quill pen. Clemmy rose and stretched his arms. He smiled a good morning to Hans.

"Look here, Clemmy, I've made you a word list. To take home with you. You can practice by writing with a stick in the sand," Hans said with enthusiasm. "I'll come visit you in five days, if you like."

And so it was arranged. Clemmy took the scroll, bid farewell to Hans and began the long walk home.

Johann's Chair

"I like the goats," Marbelard said, sitting at the table with Clemmy. Jude was outside sitting by Fedde's grave, and Clemmy was studying the paper on which Brother Hans had written a list of words in two columns. Beside each word was a drawing of what the word meant. Sun, moon, stars, tree, man, woman, child and so on. He was paying no attention to Marbelard.

"I like getting the water."

In fact, Marbelard was a champion at water getting. Something about water seemed to please him. He waded in the stream, jumping from rock to rock with unexpected agility considering his left leg was misshapen and stiff. He often looked at his reflection in the still pool, sometimes making his hair wild, making grotesque faces. Clemmy watched him do this one day and wondered what Marbelard thought of himself. He wondered if Marbelard was experimenting with ugly faces as a way of discovering his own true appearance, hoping to find it somewhere on this side of ugliness. And perhaps the graceful leaps on river stones were his way of canceling out his deformities. Less and less Clemmy saw the humped shoulder, the tilted head and withered hand. More and more he saw Marbelard's heart and curiosity and imagination.

"Clemmy."

"Yes? You said something but I wasn't listening."

"Are you going to be the Pope?" Marbelard asked.

"Um . . . no. Just a farmer, I think."

"Can't a farmer be the Pope? I know that Jesus was a carpenter because Johann, in the village, said so. And Johann had a chair made by Jesus and he would sell it to me for six pennies," Marbelard said earnestly, aiming one eye at Clemmy.

"He lied to you. He just wanted your money," Clemmy said.

"I didn't have six pennies and it wasn't a very good chair. I thought Jesus was not so good at chairs, but I still wanted it."

"You should want better things than Johann's old chair, Marbelard," Clemmy said seriously.

"What should I want?" Marbelard asked slowly. It was not the question of a fool.

"I think you should want to be happy and you should want to enjoy your life. You should want a full belly and a warm place to sleep. And a friend to be with."

"I want to be handsome," Marbelard said with feeling. "And I want to look right. My hands and my legs." His head bobbed and his tongue worked in his cheek. His bidirectional eyes misted with tears, working together at last, in sadness. Clemmy reached across the table and put his hand on Marbelard's shoulder.

"Well, I can understand why you would want that, but I still think there are better things to want." Clemmy smiled reassuringly. "Maybe you are like Johann's chair. Not very well made but still quite valuable all the same. If I had a brother, Marbelard, I would want him to be just like you. And I hope you will stay with us."

"All right."

"All right?"

"Yup." Marbelard nodded and bobbed.

The Riddle Sign

Clemmy spent any spare moment studying the Latin. Jude and Marbelard listened to him recite, and soon they could follow along. Marbelard especially liked the rolling syllables of the mysterious words. When he was off by himself, he would recite aloud, copying Clemmy, and then he would laugh. He spoke the words with dignity and pointed his good finger for emphasis.

Brother Hans came to visit as promised, and the Latin lessons went on. As his vocabulary grew, Clemmy began to make up his own sentences, and the two men had halting (and laughing) conversations at the table. Although Jude and Marbelard couldn't understand what was being said, they sat quietly and listened. Sometimes their own names would creep into the unfathomable discussions. Clemmy said once: *"Marbelard ego redimo pro pullum vigintum!"*

This meant: I bought Marbelard for twenty

chickens. Brother Hans replied: *"Perficio ille oculus Deum, ille decies mille dignus pullum!"*

This meant: He is perfect in the eyes of God; he is worth ten thousand chickens. They smiled at Marbelard then, and he was very pleased with himself.

The last time they saw Brother Hans, he left his little Bible for Clemmy to read and study. He had every intention of returning for it, but he did not. Two weeks passed, then three, then four. Clemmy wondered what had become of him.

The summer days became longer and there was much work to do. The young goats grew horns. The eggs hatched, and when the chickens feathered out they were lodged in a small pen in the barn. They learned to roost on a suspended wooden bar and they found the small door to the barnyard where they peeped at the goats. Soon they learned to wander together like a miniature flotilla of sailing ships into the brush at the edge of the forest, grubbing for insects.

The garden grew thick and high. Brother Hans had brought some turnip seeds which were planted in a new bed. As promised, they grew very fast. Marbelard went on daily hikes in the forest for firewood. He dragged back dead branches, which were broken or chopped and stacked beside the cottage door. Clemmy made the weekly trip to the village market alone. There he saw the fisherman Stotts, Marbelard's father, wasting away, sick and sullen, trading his eggs for ale and catching no fish. The drunken man failed even to ask after his son.

One market day, at midsummer, Clemmy was surprised to find all the villagers crowded around a man on horseback.

The man dismounted and began nailing a large piece of paper to a tree. It seemed a strange thing for anyone to do. Even the horse was an unusual sight in the village.

"What's he doing that for?" someone asked.

"He's got a sword!"

"Ask him what he's doing."

"You ask him."

The crowd of people kept back and watched him work. He had a fierce appearance, with a thick brown beard and a leather helmet. He was tall and broad shouldered and did in fact have a sword hanging in a silver scabbard at his waist.

"Beg pardon, sir," the village weaver said. "What is it on the tree? Is it a sign?" Everyone hushed to hear the answer. Clemmy joined the crowd and was amazed to see that the paper had words written on it! He was too far back to read them.

"It's a sign, all right," the horseman said. His fierce face smiled at them, which had the effect of frightening them even more. He faced the crowd squarely and spoke again in a rich deep voice so that all could hear.

"It is a message from your king, King Fernholz

the Wise, to all his subjects. Read it and do what it says!" he called out. The villagers squinted to see the paper, traded confused looks and chattered.

"What does it say, then?" Karlmott the woodcutter asked.

"Yes, tell us what it says," said another.

"We didn't know we had a king," someone called out.

The big man frowned, which silenced the crowd. He turned and looked at the tree. All eyes followed his to the sign. He pointed at the bottom-most word, turned and spoke again in his loud voice.

"Here. You see here it says Fernholz of Mulberia. That's the name of your king."

"Yes? That's good. We follow you, sir," Karlmott said. Everyone could tell that he was about to make some joke at the big man's expense. "But what exactly does the King say? Above his name there." He fluttered his eyelashes, and his face lit with a smile. Clemmy wormed his way to the front, where he could see the sign clearly. It was in Latin.

"Fernholz the Wise, it says," the big fellow repeated, growing nervous. "It's a royal proclamation, and you must obey," he said, preparing again to mount the horse.

"Yes, yes, we know that," Karlmott insisted, "but just a few of us here, just one or two, are having a hard time with some of the words, you see? We get the general drift of the thing, you might say, sir, but maybe you could just touch on a few of the words. The harder ones, I mean."

Snickers played through the crowd. People began to jab elbows and laugh behind their hands. Clemmy read the sign and thought about it for a moment, and then he too smiled broadly.

"I just put up the signs. That's my job, and I haven't got time to chitchat," the man said gruffly. He was obviously embarrassed.

"But we can't read it!" Karlmott roared. "And so you have to read it to us, else how can we be expected to obey?"

"I can't read!" the horseman snarled back, and the villagers burst into laughter.

"But neither can we!"

"We can't read! Ha Ha!"

Karlmott said, "If he is such a wise king, why didn't he just tell you, and then you could tell us? Wouldn't that be more sensible?" Again there was laughter, Clemmy's in the midst of it.

"Are you quite sure he is a wise king?" Karlmott goaded the man. The villagers quieted to hear the answer.

"He is a wise king," a voice answered for the beleaguered sign hanger. It was Clemmy. He spoke again. "He is wiser than many who stand before you, sir." The people murmured. Karlmott frowned.

"It's a riddle," Clemmy said. "If you can't read the sign, you don't have to obey it," he explained.

"And if this man could read it, then there would be no reason for him to hang it!" He laughed out loud. Everyone else just stared at him.

The big man walked toward Clemmy. "Can you read it?" he asked.

"I can."

"Then read it aloud for all to hear," he ordered.

"It says:

WANTED:
Someone who knows
how to read Latin.
Answer at once.
Reward offered.

King Fernholz of Mulberia."

Your King Needs You

As the crowd of illiterate villagers dispersed, the man took down his sign from the tree. He watered his horse, Birch, while Clemmy traded his cheese for flour and some fish. On the path home, the horseman introduced himself.

"I am Magnus of Near Oscarhill," he said.

He told Clemmy that the same scene had been played out at three other villages in the last two days. He was relieved to find a reader at last.

"Are you a soldier?" Clemmy asked.

"No. There are no soldiers in Mulberia, but there is some old armor and a few swords still. I've never killed anyone. I'm a shepherd," he said.

"With helmet and sword?"

"It was the King's idea. I'm the largest man in Mulberia, and the King wants everyone to believe he has a great army of huge soldiers."

"He has only a small army, then? Or a large

army with small soldiers?"

Magnus laughed. "He has no army at all! He has a thousand sheep and one horse."

"You've given away his secret," Clemmy said. The man put a finger to his lips and looked seriously at Clemmy.

"I suppose I have," he said. "But it's right for me to tell you. The Turk would never get it out of me, even if he tortured me." He said this gruffly, and Clemmy believed him.

And then he walked a few steps away from the path and cut a handful of blue and yellow wildflowers with his sword and sniffed them with pleasure. This gesture seemed utterly incongruent with his large size and frightening appearance. Even the horse seemed to stare in perplexity. Magnus' eyes were dark and wrinkled at the corners, set wide apart under great bushy brows. He was easily a foot taller than Clemmy, was barrel-chested and had enormous hands, scarred from years of sheep shearing. He lashed the flowers to his saddle, and they walked on.

"Why does King Fernholz need a reader of Latin? I mean, who wrote the sign? Why didn't the King just send for him?"

"The sign was written by the palace priest. The King ordered him to read Latin, but the man just wrote the sign, and then he ran away. King Fernholz got rather angry about it."

"Then why didn't he send for one of the monks?"

"The monks have gone. Packed and fled. The monastery is deserted."

"But why?"

"Rumors of the Turk," the soldier-shepherd said.

So, Clemmy thought, that's what became of Brother Hans. And once again he had Hans' little Bible.

"Turk makes short work of churchmen," Magnus went on. "Burns them at the stake and steals their money, that's what some say."

"And Fernholz has no army," Clemmy said. "What will he do, write the Turk a letter?"

"Ha! No, that's not it. Ha, ha! That's very funny. 'Dear Turk . . .'" The man roared with laughter. He had a tremendous loud voice.

"What, then?"

"Well, I don't know, really. King Fernholz has not got time at present to worry about the Turk. There is a matter of far more importance on his mind," Magnus said seriously.

"Which is?"

"Love, of course! The King is in love, and it takes up a lot of his time. The Turk will simply have to wait."

Clemmy remembered what Balfounder the merchant had told him about Fernholz' lady.

"And so he wants to write her love letters in Latin?"

"No, it's much more complicated than that. I

really can't explain it, but you must come at once to Mulberia."

"I have a family. And animals. And winter to prepare for," Clemmy protested. "Couldn't he come here?"

"It's not possible," Magnus said. "The King will give you rooms and food. You must obey." It was said simply, not with any malice or tone of threat. "He is your king and he needs you. Even the priests say that the first responsibility of a king is to marry and have sons. Fernholz himself says: 'A king with no sons is like a river with no water.'"

"Hmmmmm."

"You must."

"And what if the Turk comes when I am away? Who would look after my mother?"

"Bring her."

"What of my goats? And the garden?"

"Sell the goats!"

"My mother is old. It's too far for her to go."

"She can ride the horse." Magnus had an answer for every objection.

"I don't really know how to read very well," Clemmy tried.

"You must come, anyway. And that's that." The man smiled and raised his great eyebrows.

And so with Magnus' gentle insistence, the arrangements were made for Clemmy's unexpected call to service. The goats were given on loan in exchange for their milk to another homestead family. These same people were agreeable to watering and harvesting Clemmy's large garden with a promise to share the food and grain if Clemmy returned to his cottage before winter.

As it turned out, Clemmy's objections met with little support from his family. Old Jude seemed charmed by the large friendly man, and Marbelard fancied the opportunity for an adventure.

At Magnus' urging they set out on the next market day, northward through the forest. With great misgivings Clemmy turned to take a last look at his little cottage, which would, in fact, be torched by the marauding Turks before the next full moon. Not even Magnus, the largest man in Mulberia, could have stopped them.

Mulberia

For four days, Magnus took them northward, leading the horse with Jude in the saddle, while Clemmy and Marbelard walked behind. If they came across a north-going trail, they kept to it. If it turned east or west, they left it. At night they slept on the hides that the horse carried, away from any path and under tree cover. Magnus often sniffed the air for smoke, and when he smelled it, he detoured away from it.

"Best to travel unseen," he said one evening as they filled their water flasks at a small stream. This kind of talk only fueled Marbelard's sense of adventure. He became very watchful thereafter. Clemmy heard him whispering in Latin as they hiked on into hilly country far beyond even the abandoned monastery. Clemmy reckoned the monastery to be east and south. He wondered where Brother Hans had got to.

At midmorning on the fifth day they joined a

path that climbed back and forth to a heavily wooded ridge top, and there they stopped to rest. Magnus helped Jude off her mount and Birch nibbled the dense underbrush. As the horse wandered farther from the trail, Clemmy followed him away from the others.

When Clemmy returned with Birch, he found only his mother, asleep against a fallen log, and nearby, Magnus' boots. He tied off the horse and called out to Marbelard. No answer. After some searching, he found cloak and sandals at the base of a tall pine. Making his way to a clearing in the forest, he looked up to see Marbelard in the highest branches, swaying in the breeze like some great oversized bird. And then, from some distance and high overhead, came Magnus' great baritone laughter. Clemmy shook his head in wonder.

When Magnus at last returned, he said, "I nearly lost my grip in fright when I turned my eyes east and saw another man high in the branches!"

"Another man?" Jude asked.

"Marbelard," Clemmy told her. The old woman laughed.

"And what else did you see?" she asked.

"I saw that we are too far west," Magnus answered, tying on his boots.

"Are we lost?" Clemmy asked.

"No, not lost. By nightfall tomorrow we will be very close." Marbelard approached them, bobbing and smiling widely. Standing still, he swayed as though he were still in the treetops.

"And what did you see, Master Marbelard?"

"I saw Pope Magnus!"

Unlike the Turk, Magnus' sense of direction was true. They broke camp early and, as the eastern sky glowed pink, hiked along a woodcutter's path down the side of the ridge. The land ahead was rolling hillsides and wide grassy valleys that revealed small cottages not unlike the home they had left behind. By midmorning they joined a road made by pony carts and many feet. They followed the ruts north and east. Magnus quickened his pace, and Clemmy and Marbelard hurried to keep up.

Twice they met family groups going the other direction, carrying all they owned: pots and jugs and blankets and food. A small man pulled a wooden cart with his old father sitting among bags of food and hides and garden tools. A woman, his wife, walked alongside carrying two babies, one in front and one in back. She had a face full of worry and was relieved to sit and rest while the men spoke.

"We've left our home, as have many others," the man said. One of the babies began to cry. "We're taking to the woods until the war is over," he whispered.

"Has there been no call to arms?" Magnus asked.

"A call to legs, more like," the man said. "The King has said that God will save him from the infidels, though God has not saved many others. Even the palace priest has fled to the hills."

At last the road widened and turned due north, descending through a thick forest. At the base of a wooded hillside they came onto a wide treeless plain, half a mile wide and easily a mile long. At the far end was a lake, deep blue like the sky. Beyond the lake the land began to rise again. Mountain peaks stood far to the north. It was a breathtaking view. Magnus stopped the horse and pointed toward the lake.

"Mulberia lies before you," he said. "There are castle walls and two stone towers there, do you see?"

Clemmy followed Magnus' finger to a point above and west of the lake. He could just make out a gray stonework, which he had at first taken for a rocky hillside. "I see it. It's many miles yet."

"Beyond those mountain peaks is the sea, though I've never seen it. My own home is west and beyond the castle in the bare hill country where there are good pastures."

"And many sheep," Marbelard said, repeating what Magnus had told him before.

"Yes. Over a thousand sheep and many shepherds like me, though none as large. Too many sheep to hide from the Turk, I'll say."

"We shouldn't have come," Clemmy said. "We are walking into the path of a war while everyone else flees."

"King Fernholz will not force you to stay," Magnus said. Clemmy looked at Jude humming her tune in the saddle. He looked at Marbelard sitting quietly on a rock. He thought of the many miles they had traveled.

"There's no going back," he said finally. "God will have to save us as well."

King Fernholz the Fair

As the party of four crossed the treeless plain, the city wall stretched across the horizon and grew higher. The walls were made of pale white and gray stone that was quarried from the face of a granite cliff a hundred feet high. The cliff face was a half mile long and formed the protective northern boundary of the city. The great man-made wall was itself almost a mile in length, and semicircular. Either end of the wall rejoined the cliff from which the stone had been hewn to build it.

The towers of the castle rose like two gray fingers pointing at heaven—or anyway at the blue sky, if heaven was elsewhere. All the stone gave Clemmy the impression of strength and permanence. Surely a fine king must live here.

How should a king look? Wise and just, Clemmy supposed. With a golden crown and fine robe, Marbelard imagined. A king should be kingly. He should have refined speech and elegant manners.

He should be a friend to his subjects and yet command their respect. Above all, Clemmy thought, a king should be fair. He, of course, had never seen a king.

In another hour, Magnus led them through the wide wooden gates of the city of Mulberia. He talked briefly with the gatekeeper, Portnoy, whose business it was to interrogate strangers and extract from them any lively gossip. At sundown it was his duty to push the great doors shut and drop the iron bolts. He was a nervous and talkative man.

"And who would they be?" (gesturing toward Clemmy and Marbelard and Jude). "And what is their business here?"

Magnus introduced them by name. "They are loyal subjects come at the King's request," he said.

"And do you vouch for them, Magnus of Near Oscarhill?" the gatekeeper asked.

"That I do, Mr. Portnoy. And what news can you tell me about comings and goings?"

"Comings? None since I saw you last. Goings? Yes, yes, I'm afraid many are going. Half a city is out there under the pines, taking cover. Yes. So it is. Strange times, these, Magnus."

"Will you go or stay, Portnoy?" Magnus asked.

"Stay! Yes! A whole life of training at the doors, I have. The doorman of Mulberia, as you know, Magnus, is the first and last line of defense. Yes. I must be ready to close the doors. I'm staying. Portnoy is ready!" he said loudly.

Well then, at least the Turk won't hi-ho through the front door, Clemmy thought. The walls were twenty feet high and three feet thick. A narrow catwalk of stone ran along the inside near the top. He turned to look at the many stone and wooden buildings, which were built one against the next. There were hundreds of these homes curving in connected rows along the wall. Some were high, others low. Some had tile roofs. As they passed among these buildings, keeping to the main road, they saw few people about. A small group of children ran playing with a dog. Laundry could be seen hanging on lines.

"Many are working in the fields in the valley," Magnus said. "Some are running the looms or cutting wood, and many have flown, it seems." Ahead they heard shouting.

As they neared Fernholz' castle, they came upon a wide open area with a large marketplace on one side and a public well on the other. In the center, an impromptu playing field was marked off with short staves tied with bright pieces of cloth. At each end was a large wicker basket turned on its side. Along the edge of the field people stood in small groups, shouting at a dozen men running on the grassy field. Each man had a carved stick which he used to strike at a large leather ball. The ball was more or less round and wobbled to and fro among them. The game involved much laughter and falling down and no apparent strategy. As it was a warm day, they were sweating and dirty and some had removed their shirts. Clemmy saw a bit of blood here and there.

As they watched, there was a pileup at midfield. Arms and legs and sticks stuck up at odd angles, and there were grunts and groans and curses. The leather ball rolled to one side, and a tall red-bearded fellow hit it with his stick and hobbled after it toward one of the wicker baskets. He was overtaken by another man (Waltur, a weaver who had invented the game and made the leather ball himself). Both men jabbed at the ball. The bearded one struck Waltur across the shins with his stick. Clemmy heard the man cry out in pain and the other turned and guided the ball into the basket.

On the sidelines a cheer went up and the bearded man waved his arms joyfully.

"Cheat!" Waltur yelled, rubbing his shins. "You cheat. It's not fair! He struck me. You saw him!" The spectators hissed at him. Marbelard laughed out loud.

The men on the field helped each other up and walked together, laughing, toward the basket. There they tossed the sticks into a pile. Waltur the weaver threw his own stick down in disgust and stormed away without another word. The others drifted away. A few limped and nursed minor injuries. The man who had hit the ball into the basket waved at Magnus and limped toward where they stood.

"Hello, Magnus," the man said warmly. He

looked at Jude and then Clemmy. Finally his eyes came to rest upon Marbelard, who bobbed and smiled.

"You cheated!" Marbelard said happily. The man grinned at him.

"Well, sir," he said, "you don't know the rules, so I'm afraid you are mistaken." He winked at Magnus.

Marbelard was not convinced. He shook his head.

"There is one rule above all rules," the man went on, "and that is to obey God and your king. It was God who grew the stick, and it was the King who bade me stroke Waltur's legs so that I might score a point for God, King and country."

"If I were King," Marbelard said slowly, straightening himself, "I would give you ten lashes for cheating and fine you a hundred pennies!" And then he ducked his head and smiled at Clemmy.

"Well, lucky for me that you are a fool and I am King." This he said with kindness and raised his red eyebrows at Marbelard. Huge Magnus laughed long and loud. His rich laughter echoed off the castle walls.

The East Tower

Magnus wasted no time in shedding his armor and returning to his simple shepherd cottage. He had had enough of soldiering and sign hanging. He had faithfully performed the King's errand, and now he was done with it.

The sun was setting as Clemmy, Jude and Marbelard entered the great castle. The King promised them dinner would be ready shortly, and he left them in the care of a servant who showed them to rooms with wide, soft beds. After washing away the dust from the trail, Jude tested one of the beds and fell fast asleep.

Clemmy sat in the King's dining room, on one side of a long wooden banquet table. Before him was a plate piled with small new potatoes and roasted game hen baked brown and tender. The pleasing odor filled his nostrils. He held in his hand an ornate silver fork that a plump servant girl had set beside the plate. She had returned twice, once with embroidered napkins and again with a pitcher of wine, then bowed shyly and disappeared.

Across from Clemmy, Marbelard wasted no time with a fork, using his fingers instead. He smacked his lips with pleasure.

Clemmy looked about him to memorize the grand room. There were colorful tapestries hanging on the walls and a huge fireplace at one end. Soft chairs and an upholstered bench were positioned in front of the fireplace. A great shield and battle lance were attached to the wall above the mantel. As Clemmy bit into a potato, a carved wooden door opened and the King, Fernholz the Wise, entered the room. He wore a deep-red robe. He had washed his hair and brushed the tangles from it, and on his head now was a silver crown set at a jaunty angle. The King crossed to the table, favoring his left leg. He folded his arms and smiled widely.

"Master Clemmy, eat up your dinner. There's much to be done. I've been waiting weeks for you!"

"Yethir," Clemmy mumbled through the potatoes. He tasted the tender game hen and looked up through his mop of hair at the King, who took the seat beside Marbelard. He saw that King Fernholz had many freckles to match his red hair, and a red beard that was wispy and graying, though he was still a young man. High on one cheek, below his eye, he had a wart. It had the appearance of being an elevated freckle, above its peers: king freckle. Clemmy tasted the sweet grape wine. Fernholz drummed his fingers on the slab of a table.

When the meal was reduced finally to a stack of bones, Marbelard pushed his plate away and laid his head on his arms. Clemmy reached across and gave him a gentle shake. Marbelard took some bread for Jude and bobbed away to his soft bed. When he had gone, the King spoke again.

"Where, may I ask, did you learn to read? It's an unusual talent for a farmer."

Clemmy told him about the wonderful letters of indulgence, about his father, Fedde, about Brother Hans and his Latin lessons. Fernholz listened with interest to Clemmy's tale about buying Marbelard for twenty chickens.

"His eyes look east and west at the same time," the King said. "And he has a spoiled foot from birth. I understand this, Clemmy, because my own left leg has been wrong since my mother, the queen, gave me birth. As a boy I grew up lame. I watched my parents trying to replace me with a suitable heir to the throne, or so I imagined. But they had girls. And the girls were no better. They were weak, and they died as ugly little babies." The King sighed and scratched his red beard.

"My father spent his life building the great wall, and when the last stone was in place, he died and was buried with his many little daughters in the churchyard." He pointed absently toward the east.

It was a sad story. Clemmy imagined Fernholz the lame boy waiting always for a brother to take his place. Fate had not ordained it, however.

"And now," Fernholz went on, "it is I who must look to my heirs, of which there are none. And that, my friend, is why I need a reader."

"A reader? Why?"

"Because a king with no sons is like a ship with no sails. Come with me." The King rose and limped toward the wooden door from which he had entered. Clemmy rose quickly, circled the long table and hurried after.

The door led to a short hallway and then up a series of wooden stairways. Oil lamps provided the only light. Up and up they climbed. Each stairway reached a small landing, turned and continued upward. Following the lame King, Clemmy had to hurry not to lose sight of the swirling red robe ahead of him.

Finally the long ascent ended. The last steps widened onto a circular stone floor, bathed in moonlight from windows all around. Clemmy's eyes adjusted slowly to the deepening twilight. He followed the King to one of the window openings, looked out and caught his breath in surprise.

The city lay far below them, in miniature from the great height. They were, Clemmy realized, in one of the high towers of the castle. In the moonlight he could see the full length of Fernholz' father's wall.

He saw the flat plain reaching far beyond that and the dark hills through which he had traveled with Magnus.

"This is the East Tower, built by my grandfather," Fernholz said. "Look that way." He pointed east. Inside the far eastern end of the wall were many high trees and fine homes with tiled roofs.

"The richest of my people live in those houses, which were built by my great-grandfather."

"They are beautiful homes, all right," Clemmy agreed.

"And it is from there, Clemmy, that the future of Mulberia will come. For there, living in the endmost house, is a lady so fair, so perfectly beautiful and refined that she was born to be a queen." He spoke honestly and with emotion.

"And you have asked her to marry you?"

"I have!"

"Well then, congrat—"

"She said no!"

Clemmy didn't know what to say. The King spoke again.

"I must have her, Clemmy. I simply must! Her name is Lady Libby. She is young and has a stubborn streak to match her beauty, I'm afraid. I have given her fine gifts. She doesn't care. I have had great dances in her honor and she cares not. I have even stood beneath her balcony, Clemmy, with arms wide in supplication and sung her a love song, though I'll admit I don't have a great singing voice and someone, not her of course, but someone threw a cabbage at me. At me! Their King! But I found out who. It was Libby's cousin Molina. I had to jump to avoid being hit by the cabbage!"

Fernholz practically wept in his excited retelling of the awful experience. Clemmy gazed down from the tower at the dark city. He was glad that Marbelard was not present to make odd remarks, or laugh out loud. Such an earnest king! But then, shouldn't a king be earnest?

"Perhaps," he said delicately, "perhaps it is not in God's plan that you should marry this woman. Someone else, maybe?"

"She has destroyed me, Clemmy. Her graceful and dignified rejection of my proposal has ruined me! And everyone knows about it because there are no secrets in Mulberia. Everyone talks about everyone else and there are gossips on every corner."

"But you stood singing by her house. Of course they know."

"I did, in fact. But who could resist a singing king? I must have this woman, Clemmy. I love her like a madman."

Clemmy was much moved by the King's obvious suffering. He wondered if he himself would ever love a woman enough to risk appearing foolish to win her. He saw Fernholz lose himself in his own thoughts and he saw a solitary tear circumvent the wart and glide down the King's face. At that moment, Clemmy felt the humiliation as if it had been he himself dodging cabbages.

"Has the lady actually given you a reason for refusing you?"

The King blushed slightly and then sighed. "Yes. Yes, she has. It's something about my . . . uh . . ."

"Your what?"

"My wart!" He pointed to his wart. It was a very small wart, really. Nobody likes warts, naturally, but it was not so bad as some. Not a terrible wart. Just a wart.

"There! Now I've told you everything. She finds fault with me, Clemmy, because of my wart. Probably nowhere in all of Europe is there a king who hasn't got some little flaw," he protested. "A double chin or a big nose or a bald head. Bad manners or big feet or something!"

"I will help you," Clemmy promised. "But how will a reader of Latin help?"

Fernholz composed himself and faced his new friend. "Because"—the King took on a sly look and raised one finger—"because, Clemmy, I have a plan."

"Begging the King's pardon, sir . . ."

"Yes?"

"What about the Turk?" Clemmy said quickly. "Half the people have fled, I'm told."

King Fernholz waved the question away impatiently. "The Turk, the Turk. God will protect

Mulberia from the Turk, if that's His will."

"But your own priest has flown, sir. In fear of the Turk."

"Yes, he did. And he won't be welcomed back, I can tell you. I'll get a new priest. One who's not a coward."

"So you're not worried, then, about the Turk?"

"What's to worry about the Turk? He has very poor sense of direction. The Turk couldn't find his own bottom with both hands at high noon!" Fernholz laughed. Clemmy wondered if that was one of his wise sayings.

"I have more important things to worry about," the King said, fingering the little wart.

"What is the plan?" Clemmy asked, after a moment.

"I want you, Clemmy, to go and talk to Libby first thing in the morning. I always seem to say the wrong things."

"What should I say to her?" Clemmy asked.

Fernholz began to pace back and forth excitedly. "Tell her I'm removing the wart!"

"But how?"

The King turned and rubbed his hands together. "I'll tell you tomorrow," he said with a wink and stomped away down the stairs. Clemmy yawned, took one more bird's-eye view of Mulberia and went to find his bed.

Shiefelbine

In the morning Clemmy was awakened by Marbelard's laughter. Marbelard was sitting on his bed, making faces into a small round mirror with an ivory handle. As Clemmy rubbed the sleep from his eyes, his mother entered the room. She was wearing a pretty pale-blue robe, a gift from the King.

"Look at this handsome picture," Marbelard said, handing Jude the mirror. Jude looked into the glass and shook her head.

"All I see is a hungry old woman," she teased.

"Food!" Marbelard cried.

"Food! Yes. Now! Get up, Clemmy!" She swatted her son.

They had breakfast together in the long dining room. Jude was delighted by the silver spoon she was given to eat her porridge with. After the meal, with a secretive smile, she slipped the spoon into her pocket.

King Fernholz himself brought a steaming pot of

coffee, said his good mornings and joined them at the table. He had arranged a tour of the city, he said, for Jude and Marbelard. Magnus would be their tour guide.

Leaving the others, Clemmy and the King went through several doorways and emerged into the morning sunlight. They walked into a wide garden. Here was the King's well. Many flowers grew in beds along a tall hedge. In the center was a small stone fishpond circled by perfect green grass. A small old man was sitting on a bench by the pond. He was wearing a tattered purple robe and was slumped forward, nodding in sleep. The King stopped and pulled Clemmy to one side. He spoke softly.

"The man you see there, Clemmy, is some kind of priest who has spent most of his life living in a cave. He came here the same day our own coward priest disappeared," Fernholz said with significance. "Just as Portnoy was closing the city gates, he appeared and rapped on the doors with his cane. He told the doorman he had been sent by God to save the King!"

"To save the King?"

"Me, of course!"

"Of course," Clemmy echoed.

"Since then he's hardly said another word, except to say that he needed someone worthy who could read Latin. He's got his book of spells there, in that filthy old bag he carries with him. Every day he just sits by the fishpond sleeping in the sun. And now,

Clemmy, you have come to help him save me!" Fernholz beamed with pleasure and clapped Clemmy on the back.

"From the Turk?" Clemmy asked.

"To save me from despair," the King said. "To save me from the Lady Libby's rejection, to make her love me as I love her, Clemmy, for despair is far worse than even the Turk. And you must help him."

"Why doesn't the man read his own spells?"

"Because he is blind," the King whispered in Clemmy's ear.

They walked into the garden on a stone pathway bordered by red and yellow tulips. Clemmy saw honeybees going from blossom to blossom. As they neared the fishpond, the old man straightened and tilted his head, listening to the approaching footsteps. He nodded, as if his ears told him everything. Fernholz and Clemmy stopped in front of the bench.

"At last you have brought me a reader." He spoke evenly. His voice was weak with age but had a tone of certainty and relief. His unseeing eyes swept across Clemmy like torchlight, seeing everything and nothing in a single glance.

"I have done so," Fernholz announced happily. "Master Clemmy, a farmer and a student of the monks, has come to help us. This, Clemmy, is Shiefelbine."

"Leave us!" the man exclaimed. Fernholz, jumping in surprise, lost his balance and nearly fell into the pond. Then, gathering his composure, he rolled his eyes and smiled. He leaned toward Clemmy and whispered, "Save me quickly!" and then he hobbled away toward the castle door.

Clemmy pulled up a small wooden bench and sat opposite Shiefelbine. The old man stroked his beard and breathed deeply the fragrant garden air. Clemmy, who was at first frightened at the sight of him, relaxed unaccountably. He was curious, of course, but unafraid. Shiefelbine seemed to sense this.

"I saw you coming, boy," he said quietly.

"But how?" Clemmy asked in astonishment.

"There are many kinds of seeing," Shiefelbine said.

"Did you live in a cave, really?"

"I did. I was unworthy of the light. I ate moss and toads and drank the sour water and waited a lifetime for another chance. And then I woke up one morning on the stone floor of my dwelling with a clear and certain command to come to this sunny place and save a foolish king. One hears and one must obey. God has spoken!"

Clemmy wondered if it was madness or holiness that brought the man. And he could see for miles but was blind! Toads? Could a man live a lifetime eating toads?

"You ate toads?"

"I ate toads, yes. I ate ten thousand toads

and"—he paused and appeared to be counting on his fingers—"and seventeen snakes!" Clemmy made a horrible face.

"And I said a prayer before each one. And then my prayer was answered and here I am. Maybe it was the toads' prayers that were answered, I don't know! I am old and stupid and about to die, but before I die I will save your King."

"From the Turk?" Clemmy asked.

"From whatever," Shiefelbine answered. "From whatever it is that he needs saving from I will save him. So. There it is."

In the parlance of modern times, Shiefelbine's promise could be compared to a blank check. Or a coupon: good for one king saving (from whatever), by a blind old man who eats toads. So. There it is.

"I might die any day, lad, so we have to get on with it. Are you ready?" Shiefelbine made odd faces with his lips. He puckered into kiss position, then sucked his lips inside and made a sort of low humming noise that usually ended with a whistled bird call.

"I might die tomorrow or I might die next week. I might die lying down or maybe even standing up! I might die right here on this bench. Who knows? Look at this!" he demanded, loosening the string on an old furry bag.

The bag appeared to have mange. The fur was falling off under Shiefelbine's bony fingers. He pulled it open and began withdrawing bits of bone, small pouches of powder, dried roots and moss. Clemmy was half afraid he would pull out a snake. The old man piled these treasures on the bench, making whistling noises all the while. Finally, he pulled from the bag a book with a black cover, set it gently aside and swept all the other odd items back into the bag. The air hung with cave dust until a light breeze swirled it away.

Watching the old man, Clemmy wondered again about madness and holiness. He wondered if being saved by Shiefelbine might actually be worse than being killed by someone else. He was curious about the tattered old book, however.

Shiefelbine blew the dust from the book and wiped the front cover with the sleeve of his robe, revealing a title in gold letters:

EN SUPPLICO MIRABILIS

"Do you know what it means?" Shiefelbine asked, holding up the book.

"I think it means Marvelous Prayers," Clemmy answered.

"That's right!" Shiefelbine cackled loudly and stamped one bare foot. "But before you look at the book, you have to know about prayers, Master Clemmy. And I will teach you! But we must hurry, because I might die any second. I might die before lunch!"

Heaven's Back Door

At the same time Shiefelbine was blowing the cave dust off his old book, Portnoy the doorman was just opening the city gates, and more people of Mulberia were hastening away to hide in the forest. By the doorman's count, there were very few left inside the walls.

Off to the south, twenty-nine thousand Turks on horseback galloped behind Suleiman's red flag, swinging scimitars, lusting for an enemy worthy of their murderous blades, riding hard into the foreign pastures, villages and churches that lay in their haphazard path, first east, then west, always north.

Many miles east a column of men, the monks of St. Euchre, walked through the forest, leading the pony on whose back the supply of food grew ever lighter. The monks were on a forced diet of Brother Hans' prize turnips. Morale among them was low, and their singing had not improved.

One might pause to compare a turnip diet to a

toad diet. They have, as it happens, nearly identical amounts of calories and vitamins. A large toad has no more and no less ability to sustain a holy man's meager existence than an average European turnip. When accompanied by clean water and cautious thankful prayer, it is only just enough to maintain daily penance and simple devotions.

Which brings us naturally enough to Shiefelbine's prayer book, stowed for unnumbered years in his ratty old bag. Clemmy paid close attention in case the man died momentarily, as predicted.

"Listen!" Shiefelbine commanded and wagged a finger at his young pupil. "There are three kinds of prayer. First there is bad prayer. Bad prayer is of three varieties. Are you listening?"

"Yes sir," Clemmy said. He hadn't imagined it was so complicated.

"Bad prayer may be prayer which is prayed by bad people. Or bad prayer may be prayed by good people asking for bad things. Or by good people asking for things of little importance like good weather or smooth sailing and so on. Bad prayers never even hit the mark! Ha! They fly right past heaven and zoom into the universe looking for some silly god to catch them." Shiefelbine illustrated: left hand, heaven; right hand, bad prayers winging away. Clemmy watched the old hands at work.

"Ha, ha! Not even close! Get it?"

"Yes sir."

"Next, my boy, there is perfect prayer, which blows into heaven like a gale wind, well expressed and worthy of being heard, if not always answered. These are the prayers of the great healers and holy men, the prayers of lovers and sometimes children. They are powered by their clarity and singleness of purpose. They are direct and unambiguous and they strike a balance between great need and great humility. The words are respectful and beseeching, propelled by the purity of the sender, guided by the intensity of the emotions. They blow into heaven like a hot wind."

He filled his lungs with air and blew. Clemmy felt himself doing the same.

"And there is a third kind of prayer that I must tell you about. Imperfect prayer. These prayers are borne with a similar force of pious sincerity, prayers of desperate need offered up by good people, but they are lacking in precision, you might say. They are misarranged and ungrammatical. They are mispronounced and poorly phrased or even hysterical." His hands waved about wildly.

"While perfect prayers fly straight and true, ringing the great bell of heaven and marching like an army of saints into the ears of the Almighty, imperfect prayers are like orphan children rapping on heaven's back door with spoons, raising a racket, pushing open the door and rushing forward in their rags. These imperfect prayers, Clemmy, are the most powerful of all prayers. But because of their imperfections, they almost never produce perfect results."

Shiefelbine became silent for a long moment. He shook his old head and sighed. Clemmy was surprised to see tears well up in his sightless blue eyes. There are many kinds of seeing, Clemmy remembered, and Shiefelbine was seeing some tragic event in his own past. It must have been very sad indeed to drive him into a cave for a lifetime and still cause him to weep. He waited in respectful silence for Shiefelbine to snuffle his nose and go on. The man picked up his old book and fanned its yellowed pages.

"The prayers in this book are imperfect prayers, boy. They are the most powerful prayers in the world."

He reached forward his hand and Clemmy carefully accepted *En Supplico Mirabilis.* He opened it on his lap and saw the Latin words, neatly written, filling every page. Some pages were torn, others water marked but all could be read. He ran his eyes over the sentences, slowly, wondering about the meaning of many of the words.

"With these powerful prayers, and with your help, we shall save your King." Shiefelbine pointed one bony old finger at Clemmy.

"You are the reader, Clemmy. God is waiting to hear from you!"

The Book of Imperfect Prayer

No matter which god you believe in, no matter if you live in a cave or a castle or a tent, no matter if you are noisy and talkative or tongue-tied and silent, you are only allotted your own share of words in one lifetime. To these words, once you are dead and buried, could be given a number—no more and no less. Some people have a bigger number than others.

Shiefelbine's own share of words was nearly used up. He gave Clemmy no further explanation about his imperfect-prayer book because it was rather a complicated story and he was wisely unwilling to use up so many of his last words telling it. Time was growing short, and every word counted precipitously closer to his own total.

What follows, using as few precious words as necessary, is the tale of *En Supplico Mirabilis*.

A full century before King Fernholz had his crisis of love, there was held in northern Iberia a council which became known in history as the Grand Council of Prayer. There assembled all the holy men from the entire continent and beyond. These were the devout, the amazing and the profound—the living saints and miracle men who were champions of the True Faith. They assembled to share their powerful prayers with each other. Fifty men each spoke seven prayers and a roomful of priests and monks recorded the words on paper so that multiple copies of a book could be made.

Great pious oaths were spoken by each man in turn, and the scribes dipped their quill pens again and again to keep up. As the holy men addressed the Almighty, there was no interrupting them or asking them to slow down. The words flew wildly onto the paper. When a great prayer finally reached its climax—the amen—a loud base chorus of amens rose like applause and echoed around the chamber.

One of the writers was a simple parish priest, a graybeard from the far north country named Rexroath of Carlsbud. But he was hard of hearing. Sound came to Rexroath in a muffled, far-off sort of way, so he had to strain constantly to hear. Like the others, he wrote quickly with his pen, but when he didn't quite hear the prayer, he became a nuisance by interrupting the others, saying, "What? What was that?"

The other priests became irritated and shushed him again and again. Rexroath did the best he could.

When he returned to his own country, he rewrote the prayers neatly and had them bound in a leather book. By agreement of the Grand Council, the book was to be called *En Supplico Mirabilis*, which means *The Book of Marvelous Prayers*. Rexroath of Carlsbud had this name printed on the cover of his own book, but as you might guess, his version of the prayers was different from all the others. Rexroath omitted whole lines occasionally, and many of the words were incorrect, out of place or misspelled.

Not long after the book was bound, Rexroath had an opportunity to use it. His country suffered a terrible drought. No rain fell for months, and the crops on which their lives depended dried up. There was no harvest. The village granary was empty, and people began to starve. Rexroath turned to *En Supplico Mirabilis*. He knelt on a dusty road and spoke a prayer for rain. Even before he finished, the sky darkened with storm clouds. The rain fell in sheets without ceasing for a week, two weeks. The country was flooded and many perished. The marvelous prayer book survived.

His second opportunity came several years later when a childless couple sought Rexroath's help. Again he turned to *The Book of Marvelous Prayers*. He prayed that the barren woman would conceive, which she did. The child, named Rotney, was born exactly nine months later. The parents rejoiced. In the twilight of his years, the elderly priest saw the boy grow wild and uncontrollable. At the age of ten Rotney set fire to Rexroath's little church and laughed as it burned. The priest perished in the fire. But not his dangerous prayer book, which was found inside a small chest in the rubble. The book was sent to the monastery at St. Clair, where, over time, similar lopsided episodes took place. The prayers did work miracles, but there were always unpredictable side effects. They were imperfect prayers, the most powerful kind. Finally, the friars at St. Clair locked the book away inside Rexroath's fire-charred chest. And that's where it should have stayed.

A Wedding With Darkness

En Supplico Mirabilis reappeared finally on a cool spring day nearly thirty years later. It was the day before Shiefelbine's wedding. The young groom, barely twenty years old, was the son of a rich Danish merchant. Lord Wencel, Shiefelbine's father, had arranged that his son would marry the daughter of a rich banker. The arrangement would be to Lord Wencel's advantage in terms of business. Young Shiefelbine was agreeable to the match, as was the banker's daughter Moira. That is, until they were allowed to meet (with chaperones, of course) a few days before the wedding.

The blushing Moira bowed to her betrothed in a finely appointed sitting room at her father's estate. At the moment she lowered the veil that covered her face, time stopped for Shiefelbine, with a silent crash. The bride-to-be was not a great beauty. She was not at all the lovely maiden Shiefelbine had imagined. She was not even what you could call plain. She was ugly! Eyes too close together, nose like a beak, skin pockmarked, teeth crooked, large jawed. She was horse-faced and overweight and big footed. Shiefelbine, stunned though he was, bowed like a proper young gentleman.

The brief conversation they were permitted convinced the boy that Moira was a lady indeed, subtle and charming, modest and intelligent. But still, that night, in his own chambers, the immature Shiefelbine agonized about his unhappy fate. There was no changing the wedding arrangements—it would be scandalous and cruel. Because of his wounded pride he could not sleep. He considered killing himself but couldn't seriously face such nasty business. He considered running away, but he had neither the means nor the courage. He considered pretending to be sick. He coughed experimentally into his hands, growing red-faced with shame.

The following morning Shiefelbine had one last desperate thought. He might beg to join the monks and be celibate (no wife at all, ever). He dressed and stole away to the St. Clair monastery and confessed his unhappiness to the old abbot, Bernard.

Bernard listened quietly to Shiefelbine's selfish lament, drumming his knobby fingers on his knees and thinking all the while about the generous donations that Lord Wencel, Shiefelbine's father, made to the monastery. Bernard would not interfere with the wedding and risk angering Lord Wencel. On the other hand, he knew that Wencel's fortune would one day become Shiefelbine's fortune. He determined to help the unhappy groom. Bernard needed a miracle, and time was too short to rely upon ordinary prayers. He had Rexroath's fire-blackened chest brought to his chambers.

In *The Book of Marvelous Prayers* he found a prayer for beauty, a prayer designed to convince heaven to transform a hideous person into a healthy and handsome person. It was originally composed to heal lepers. Bernard studied Rexroath's fine, flowing penmanship for some obvious flaw but found none. He was frightened by the book's power, but he believed he was doing good. He made the sign of the cross with his hand, gave Shiefelbine *En Supplico Mirabilis* and instructed him to read the prayer aloud on the night before his wedding. Bernard watched as Shiefelbine walked back to the city with an energetic stride and high hopes.

Shiefelbine cheerfully endured the final wedding preparations, telling no one his secret. He was fitted with a fine embroidered wedding robe, purple and white. He was toasted at a banquet held in his honor. At last the night before the wedding came.

Sitting before a single candle behind his locked bedroom door, Shiefelbine opened the dusty old book and studied the Latin phrases in the prayer for beauty. He rehearsed silently in the flickering candle-light.

Across the city, his bride Moira was just whispering her own going-to-bed prayers. She added to them
a plea that her husband would be kind and wise and
good. As old Shiefelbine told it now, these prayers
went wide of the mark, did not ring the bell of
heaven, did not tug on the sleeve of the Almighty.
Moira wasted about a hundred words of her own allotment, and then she went to bed.

Kneeling in his chamber, Shiefelbine took a deep
breath and spoke the words of the prayer aloud. As
his voice rose with passion and his hands reached up
to heaven, his heart filled with a glowing certainty of
success. His young eyes brimmed with tears, and just
as he spoke the final amen, the Lord God blew out
the candle. Or so Shiefelbine imagined. In the black-
ness of his dark room he stumbled to his bed.

Whether a prayer is answered for good or ill, or
not at all, people must endure the results as they
come, with joy and thanksgiving or with darkness
and despair. Shiefelbine's darkness began the next
morning when a pink and golden sunrise found no
entrance into the boy's eyes. Imagining it still night,
he lay awake in his bed waiting for first light, any
light. But no light came that day or any of the next
days. No sun or moon or candle or lamp could pene-
trate the darkness. He was blind. No physicians
could heal him, no drops or ointments had any
power over his suddenly sightless eyes.

Being blind, he was cheated of the vision of beauty that his imperfect prayer had created. Moira awakened on her wedding day transformed. Her hair had softened and gleamed about her radiant perfect skin. Her features had shifted and straightened and organized themselves into a portrait of loveliness. Her figure slimmed, her feet shrank and her bosom lifted. Her miraculous bloom became the talk of the city, a gift from God. But in spite of her glorious beauty she would be forever invisible to Shiefelbine.

The wedding was postponed while useless doctors fussed over the boy, but there was no improvement. Months passed and then a year. On the first anniversary of the scuttled wedding Shiefelbine dressed again in his sad wedding robes, stowed the imperfect-prayer book in a fur-lined bag and tap-tapped his way out of the city. He walked where his feet would take him, waded through streams and stumbled through brambles, sleeping when he was tired, for day and night meant nothing to him.

He became filthy and ragged and thin with hunger. He cared nothing for his life and determined at last that he should find a soft bit of grass to die on. And then another small miracle happened.

As he walked slowly across a stony hillside, he was surprised to feel a small hand slip into his own! Shiefelbine was afraid to speak lest he break the spell, and so he walked hand in hand with the small person who led him to a cave in a rock wall, helped him sit on a mossy stone and put a piece of bread into his hand. A child's voice said, "Stay here. I'll come back." This unexpected kindness unplugged Shiefelbine's tear ducts; a rain of tears streamed from his sightless eyes and fell onto his spoiled robes.

The little girl did come back. She brought food and sometimes she sang Shiefelbine a high-pitched hymn, which she had learned at her village church. She may have imagined him a holy man or a wandering saint. Shiefelbine grew a long beard and lived alone in his cave. His only contact with humans was the little girl, who eventually became a big girl, a mother and, finally, a middle-aged woman. Her life-saving visits became further apart. On her last visit she again took his hand and gave it a squeeze. It was good-bye, Shiefelbine knew. And so he listened carefully to her fading footsteps, to record them in his memory. He said a prayer for the woman's safety, and then he went on waiting for God to give him a second chance. After many years, God gave him Fernholz the Lame.

What Have You Brought?

Schiefelbine did not die before lunch, but he did fall deeply asleep after eating some soup that the King's last remaining kitchen helper brought for him.

Clemmy gently laid the old miracle book on the bench and left the garden through a side gate. He walked around the great stone castle and felt himself drawn in the direction of the fine houses he had seen from Fernholz' tower the night before.

He passed the stickball field, passed the royal stable, home to only one horse, named Birch. Next he crossed through a deserted marketplace and joined a fine brick-and-mortar sidewalk that curved its way down a grassy hillside and through a grove of trees alive with songbirds. The singing birds, Clemmy noticed, were oblivious to human affairs such as the dreaded Turk or unrequited love. This was a comforting thought.

Emerging from the grove Clemmy saw flowerbeds rich with bloom and wide lawns that circled many high stone houses. From the King's tower he had seen their moonlit roofs and stone chimneys. Close up in daylight, he could see they were homes of great beauty, with balconies and arching doorways. He couldn't help thinking of his own rough little cottage, a poor cousin to these fine chiseled houses. Clemmy wondered if the people who lived in them were equal to their grandeur. And then he thought of the strange Shiefelbine living a lifetime in a cave. Homes, he thought, have a way of shaping the people who live in them.

There were more citizens about than he had seen in the humble workaday section of the city. A woman was hanging clothes from a line—fine woolen garments, embroidered and colorful. A man on a ladder was repairing a wooden shutter. Clemmy walked toward the man's house.

"Good day, sir," Clemmy called out. The man stopped his work and looked down.

"And who might you be? I've never seen you before."

"I am Clemmy, a friend of Magnus'."

"Aye, I know Magnus, but I know no Clemmy."

"I've come to help your King," Clemmy insisted.

The man sighed and tapped again on the shutter. He shook his head and looked down again. "Do you give singing lessons?" he asked.

"I'm looking for the house of Libby. Can you help me?"

"I can, sir. There." He pointed across the path to a two-story stone building with a brick walkway and many roses. A climbing vine had attached itself to one side of the house and threaded its leafy way across a balcony. "It is the home of Chilton the trader, but he has been away to the north for many weeks. His daughter waits for his return in the care of her aunt, a proper woman. I can tell you they have bags packed and will waste no time in retreat when the gentleman arrives home."

"And what of you?" Clemmy called up to the man.

"I'm too old to hide in the trees," he answered. "I'll stay and fight with my hammer, if necessary. The King says God will protect us from the Turk."

"Thank you, sir." Clemmy left the man to his tapping and crossed to the rosy front lawn. He struck three times on the oaken door. After a moment the door latch clicked and the huge door swung inward and revealed a large woman with a white lace cap that was tied under her double chin. She wore a black woolen dress with black buttons from chin to ankle. In the darkness of the hallway, Clemmy thought for a brief moment that he stood before none other than Brother Garth!

"Have you brought the cheese?" the woman asked.

"No, I—"

"Have you brought the potatoes, then?"

"No, I have come—"

"Well, what have you brought?" she asked sharply.

Clemmy thought how to answer. He wished suddenly that he had brought something besides his curiosity.

"News," he said quickly. "I've brought a message from the King." The woman stepped forward to get a better look at him. "My name is Clemmy, and though it must sound strange, I've come to Mulberia to help your king and your people and I would like, with your permission, of course, to meet and talk with the Lady Libby, who I am told lives in this house." It was undoubtedly the longest sentence Clemmy had ever spoken. Libby's aunt planted her hands on her hips and stood squarely in the doorway.

"Talk to Libby?" She sounded suspicious.

"Yes, please. It's very urgent." He said it but he wasn't sure what he meant.

"Do you have news of Master Chilton?"

"No. I'm sorry. It's a matter that concerns King Fernholz. May I see the Lady?"

"Certainly not!" She stepped back and took hold

of the door. "He is a foolish king and has no business at this house!" The woman swung the door forcefully, and it slammed shut only inches in front of Clemmy's face. The air blew his hair back. Clemmy stared at the door.

So much for talking to Libby, he thought with a sigh. He turned to leave and saw a curtain drop quickly from one of the windows. Someone had been peeking at him.

As he walked away from the house, he was surprised to hear the door open again behind him.

"Let him come in, Auntie," Clemmy heard a voice say from behind the door.

Libby

From behind the door came whispering. He stood still and waited. The summer sun was high in the sky, shining through a dusty haze that, Clemmy observed, had not been there in the morning. The door to the house swung fully open finally and revealed the whisperers. Beside the aunt stood a young woman of rare beauty. She had long brown hair and gray-green eyes that gleamed in the sunlight that swept across her. Her dress was a simple green gown tied with a sash. She seemed perfectly elegant to Clemmy, who became suddenly shy. He bowed and then, straightening, shook the hair from his face and smiled uncertainly. The matron glared her disapproval at him.

"Pardon the intrusion, please," he began. "Are you the Lady Libby?"

"I am," she answered, returning his smile. "And who are you? I didn't hear."

"I am Clemmy, from many miles to the south. I

was sent for by King Fernholz, and I've come to help him." He realized it all must sound a little vague. As indeed it was. The matron spoke.

"Help the King? You should give him a swift boot in the royal hindquarters!"

The young lady laughed at the dour matron, whose suspicious gaze softened into a smirk. Clemmy felt his spirits lifting immediately. He also laughed. Libby was even more beautiful when she laughed.

"Auntie Lucia is known widely for her plain speaking," Libby said, raising her eyebrows as she took the woman's arm. "She takes pains not to be misunderstood, you see. It's a good quality. And her daughter, my cousin Molina, has inherited it. Please come in and meet her. Auntie, will you bring us tea?"

"We're nearly out of tea," Aunt Lucia said with a worried tone. "We're nearly out of everything."

"Surely we can manage tea for our guest."

Lucia disappeared with a sigh, and Libby ushered Clemmy into a comfortable sitting room with high southern windows. The furniture was finely uphol-stered and hand-tied lace curtains hung in the win-dows. Through a window, Clemmy saw someone he thought must be Molina, the cabbage thrower, snip-ping flowers on the back lawn.

When they were seated, Libby asked seriously, "Are we truly in danger of the marauding Turks? So many have fled the city."

"To be honest, I don't know," Clemmy answered.

"I fear the worst. The city is defenseless and the King does nothing to prepare. He thinks of marriage and his heirs, as you know."

"Yes, I do know," Libby answered, blushing.

"If Fernholz had his queen, then perhaps he could pay attention to matters of state."

"And have you come, Clemmy, to propose marriage for King Fernholz? Or to enlist me in the army to fight the Turk? You see, I would not happily be Fernholz' queen."

Aunt Lucia entered the room with a teapot and several ornamental cups. She served the tea, frowned at Clemmy and then lifted one of the windows.

"Molina!" she called. "Come for a cup of tea." She turned and looked triumphantly at Libby. She meant to have a chaperone in the room. Molina entered through a side door and carried her bouquet into the sitting room.

"Molina," Libby said, "this is Clemmy, come on the King's behalf." Clemmy bowed to the dark-haired girl, who had a devilish smile. Without taking her eyes off Clemmy, she extended the flowers to her mother, who did not accept them.

"Mother, please put them in a vase." The matron took the flowers. Molina gave her a look then with an almost imperceptible jerk of her head toward the kitchen. Aunt Lucia retreated, shaking her head and making a "hmmpf" sort of sound. Molina poured a cup and took a seat.

"Sent by King Fernholz?" she asked.

"Well, yes and no. I've really come to find out why the Lady refuses Fernholz in marriage." Clemmy watched the two young women exchange glances. There was a secret between them, he could tell. Libby spoke first.

"He is a good and wise king . . ."

"Yes he is!" Molina interrupted. "And all his subjects admire him. He has built the finest woolen mill anywhere and spent the treasury on homes for the poor. There are new wells dug and new fields cleared. No one is hungry in Mulberia." Molina stopped, slightly embarrassed.

"Molina admires our king very much," Libby said. And also threw a cabbage at him, Clemmy said to himself.

"But it is you he has chosen to marry," he said bluntly.

"Even kings make mistakes," she answered. "He should choose another. I do not wish to marry him."

"But why?" Clemmy persisted. He had a sense of Aunt Lucia lurking outside the sitting-room door (as indeed she was). Libby considered Clemmy's question. It was not so easily put into words.

"I don't know, exactly. I am flattered, of course, by his attentions, but . . ."

"But?"

"He has a wart," Libby said, looking at her feet.

"A wart? But surely . . ."

"He has a large wart. He is terribly disfigured by it," she went on.

"But . . ."

"On his cheek."

"A wart. Well, yes, he has a small wart, of course, but is it really so . . ."

"I will not marry King Fernholz," Libby insisted.

Clemmy was unsure what to say next. He looked at Molina, who smiled back and shrugged her shoulders. And so it was the wart after all that made Libby reject the King. Now Clemmy had heard it with his own ears. He and Libby looked at each other for a long moment. He felt his pulse quicken.

"Suppose King Fernholz had no wart, Lady Libby. Would you marry him then?"

Both Libby and Molina (and probably Aunt Lucia) were surprised by his question. The young women exchanged a puzzled look. Libby rattled her teacup.

"But how could such a thing happen?" Molina asked.

"Through prayer, perhaps," Clemmy said softly.

"Would you come back then and ask me?" Libby asked.

"Yes. Yes I would."

"Well . . . we would just have to see." Libby smiled, regaining her composure (and thinking it highly unlikely).

Clemmy smiled widely at the opportunity. He bid

the women good afternoon and hurried away toward the palace.

Because she was somewhat flirtatious and also because the conversation had turned quickly to King Fernholz, Molina had forgotten to mention a curious sensation she had felt while cutting flowers in the garden. For several minutes she had felt the earth vibrating beneath her feet. Along with this trembling, she had noticed, when she had lifted her head to listen, that the sky had become a dusty haze.

It was no mere meteorological event, however, no earthquake or dust bowl that caused the tremors and the haze. It was nothing less than the incipient turbulence of the ancient territorial imperative. It was the forward momentum of an ineluctable historical tide. It was the vast and relentless reverberations of theocratic adventure, the seizures and smog of social evolution.

It was the Turk.

The Changing of the Guard

I f the terrain had been more accommodating, this story might have ended on that very day, for the only things between Suleiman the Magnificent and King Fernholz the Lame were the creaking wooden city gates, which had been pushed shut by the terrified doorman, Portnoy. The Turkish force spilled out of the narrow forest road on the far side of the flat plain that lay before the city walls. It was the colorful Turkish battle flags that first caught Portnoy's eye. He stood suddenly frozen in his tracks, staring in disbelief at the mounted multitude pouring onto the plain. Up until that precise moment, life had been good to the pudgy gatekeeper and newshound. He hardly dared breathe as the cloud of dust rolled toward the city. In terror he shouldered the doors closed and dropped the heavy oaken bolt. And then he turned and fled.

He had not gone thirty paces when he rounded the stable wall and nearly knocked over Marbelard who had been shuffling about the city seeing the sights. Marbelard had begun to feel the earthly vibrations of the Turk's cavalry and he had stopped to listen, cocking his head to the south.

Portnoy yelped with surprise and stopped abruptly. Marbelard bobbed and cast his unfocussed gaze questioningly at the doorman. And then Portnoy pulled and twisted on a finger of his right hand, straining with the effort. He pulled off a ring made of silver and thrust it forward toward Marbelard.

"Here!" he insisted. "Take the ring and wear it for as long as you can!"

"What is it for?" Marbelard asked, taking it in his palm.

"It's the badge of the doorman," Portnoy said with a hasty glance back toward the gates. "It's a great honor, sir, and befitting a gentleman like yourself. You must watch the great doors and close them if there is danger!"

"But they're closed already," Marbelard said, swaying to one side and looking around the doorman.

"Yes! Your work is half done for you! See that ledge there? Near the top. From there you can watch beyond the walls." Portnoy began to walk away, backward. "You're the doorman now," he cried. "You've got the official ring!"

"But—"

"Your King needs you!" And then he turned and ran away.

Marbelard examined the ring with one eye and then the other. It was truly beautiful. He slipped it onto the index finger of his withered hand and admired it. Then, straightening himself with dignity, he shuffled toward the wooden doors and stood before them.

Slowly he climbed the steep stairway to the ledge where he could watch the Moslem horde spreading its ranks far across the plain. He saw the lines of lancers, horsemen and footmen. He saw many wagons of provisions, and he coughed quietly from the dust that hung in the air between the army and the city walls. Marbelard arched his eyebrows and spoke with courteous authority.

"Good afternoon, sir. And may I inquire what your business might be in Mulberia?"

The Wart

Back in the King's garden, Clemmy found Shiefelbine lying on his bench with one knobby old hand gripping the string to his wretched bag of treasures. Clemmy hurdled a row of flowers, ran to the bench and gave the old man a shake. There was no response.

He shook him again and cried, "Wake up, sir!" Shiefelbine, who was little more than a corpse anyway, made no response until, in desperation, Clemmy tried to pry the man's hand open. He felt Shiefelbine's grasp tighten on the string. Slowly the sleeper stirred himself back to life, sat up on the bench and began to scratch himself.

"You're alive!" Clemmy announced.

"I am?" Shiefelbine licked his lips and smiled gratefully. Clemmy was relieved.

"I'm so glad you're not dead," Clemmy said.

"Well. That's the nicest thing anyone ever said to

me," Shiefelbine said. Clemmy rolled his eyes with impatience.

"Get the book. We've got to find a prayer to get rid of the King's wart."

"Ah yes. *En Supplico Mirabilis*. A wart, you say?" He withdrew the old book from his bag and sighed heavily, remembering his own tragic loss on account of The Book of Imperfect Prayer. Maybe, he thought, things will be different this time. With some reluctance he handed over the book.

"Toward the front of the book," he directed Clemmy, "a page you will find with a crease. On that page is a prayer that ought to remove a king's wart easily. Sit down here and read it to me. Read softly, boy, for they are powerful words."

Clemmy found the page with the crease. Shiefelbine himself had folded the page on the night he prayed successfully for his bride's transformation.

"Clamor meus, Domine, ad te perveniat: non avertas faciem tuam a me."

"Yes, that's the one," Shiefelbine whispered, his blind eyes misting. "Go on. Read to the end." Clemmy read to the final amen. Most of the words he did not know.

"Now we will do it together. Read one line and then stop. I will repeat it." With some ceremony Shiefelbine stood on the bench, took several deep breaths, cleared his throat and thrust his spindly arms into the dusty sky.

Clamor meus, Domine, ad te perveniat . . .
CLAMOR MEUS, DOMINE, AD TE PERVENIAT!

Shiefelbine enlarged the words. Clemmy wondered why God was more likely to hear a prayer shouted from a bench.

Cor meum et caro mea exultant ad Deum vivum . . .
COR MEUM ET CARO MEA EXULTANT AD DEUM VIVUM!

Ego afflictus sum valde . . .
EGO AFFLICTUS SUM VALDE!

In his tower King Fernholz' eyes had shifted to the south and narrowed with annoyance at the gathering Turks on his sheep-shearing plain. So, you have found us at last, he thought. It was widely rumored that Suleiman the Magnificent had three hundred wives, and yet he had come all the way from Constantinople to interfere, the King thought, with Fernholz' own courting of the Lady Libby. It seemed so grossly out of proportion. And also quite inconsiderate.

Domine, ad adiuvandum me festina . . .
DOMINE, AD ADIUVANDUM ME FESTINA!

Oculi mei ob miseriam tabescunt . . .
OCULI MEI OB MISERIAM TABESCUNT!

And yet, Fernholz mused, if God has brought the Turk to Mulberia, there must be a good reason. Maybe they only want to ask directions. He turned and looked back to the east. Oh Libby, my darling, why must it be so difficult being King? For what is a king with no sons? A sky with no stars. A forest with no birds.

Rivi aquarum fluxerunt de oculis meis . . .
RIVI AQUARUM FLUXERUNT DE OCULIS MEIS!

Ut non derelinquat me in die tribulationis meae . . .
UT NON DERELINQUAT ME IN DIE TRIBULATIO-
NIS MEAE!

On the other hand, the King thought, there's no need to be so gloomy. For besides bringing the murderous Turk, God had also brought Shiefelbine, that very strange person, to save me. But. But! He turned back to look at the ever-widening ranks of horsemen. What if Shiefelbine saved him from the Turk but did nothing to save him from despair? It was growing ever more difficult to remain cheerful.

Nihil sani est in carne mea . . .
NIHIL SANI EST IN CARNE MEA!

Amen.

AMEN!

Shiefelbine's beseeching old arms flopped to his side. He seemed completely spent from the effort of praying. Clemmy helped him down from the bench.

"Leave me now," the man croaked. "Go and see what's become of the royal wart." He appeared to fall asleep immediately. Clemmy returned the prayer book to Shiefelbine's bag. He crossed himself then, looking up into the dusty sky, and hurried away toward the palace doors.

Inside, he made his way ever upward, assuming rightly that the King would be mooning away in his tower. The stairs seemed endless, and he panted for air as he made the final turn and staggered up the last flight of steps. As he had expected, he found Fernholz staring morosely down on his kingdom. The King turned to greet him. Clemmy struggled for his breath and studied Fernholz' face. And then he clapped his hands with joy and laughed between gasps. Then for one brief second his eyes took a glance south.

"Oh dear God!" Clemmy exclaimed. He forgot the King's melodrama and thought of his mother and of Marbelard. It was true after all. The Turk was on their doorstep!

"Oh, don't worry about them." Fernholz waved blithely toward the horde. "Tell me about your chat with Shiefelbine. What did he say to you?"

"It's gone, sir," Clemmy said, pulling his eyes away from the dreadful scene below and pointing at the King's face.

"Gone? What's gone?"

"Your wart! It's gone. Shiefelbine prayed for a miracle."

Fernholz put his hand to his cheek. His red eyebrows arched in disbelief. And then he seemed to explode with happiness. He laughed and jumped up and down. He embraced Clemmy and danced, and then he thundered away down the stairs in search of a looking glass. After several minutes, as the King charged back up the stairs, Clemmy heard the thumping of Fernholz' bad leg.

"It's gone! It's gone! You've done it! She's mine at last! She will have to marry me now." The King made happy faces into his mirror.

"What are you going to do?"

"I'm going to get married, Clemmy! And have sons!"

"No, about the Turk, I mean." Clemmy nodded his head toward the window.

"Forget the Turk!" Fernholz shouted. "I'll invite them to the wedding. All of them. But they have to bring presents!" He laughed with pleasure. And then he grew very earnest.

"Clemmy, you've got to help me."

"Yes? What?"

"Go see Libby. Tell her the wart's gone and I

await her reply to my proposal. Quickly!" The King practically pushed Clemmy down the stairs. "I'll wait here for you."

"No."

"What?"

"I'll collapse if I have to climb these stairs again."

"Oh, very well. But go! Quickly!"

News

So, less than an hour after leaving there, Clemmy was back at Libby's door. He knocked politely. After a long moment the door swung open slowly and revealed the sturdy matron, Aunt Lucia, expecting provisions, obviously disappointed. She resisted the impulse to thrust the door shut and made do with a nasty frown.

"You again?"

"A word with the young lady, please?" Clemmy tilted his head and grinned. "It's very important, madam."

"Wait here," she said scoldingly, and disappeared. When the door opened again, it was Libby who stood in the doorway. Clemmy was amazed again by her beauty. They both smiled awkwardly, and a blushing, silent moment passed.

"Master Clemmy," Libby said.

"Good day again," Clemmy began uncertainly.

"Did you forget something?" she helped him.

"I've come for the King. I mean, because he asked me to come. Just as he did this morning."

"The King came this morning?"

"No. Or yes, rather. He didn't come. I came. This morning. Just a while ago, of course. But he didn't ask me."

"He didn't ask if you came?"

"Well, no, he didn't ask me that, but he did ask me, you know, to come. As I did before." Clemmy was confusing himself. The Lady Libby was teasing him, but he didn't exactly know that, either.

"But here you are again," she laughed.

"Yes! And I have news."

"About my father?"

"No, I'm sorry."

"About the Turk, then?"

"Well, no. Although you may as well know that the Turk has arrived outside the city walls."

Libby was stunned. The mirth fell from her face. She clasped her hands together and looked very worried. What news could be more important than the impending attack?

"But that's not what I came to tell you," Clemmy said, feeling slightly foolish. "King Fernholz has lost his wart through devout prayer, and he asks you again to marry him."

The young girl gave Clemmy a very odd look. She seemed to be studying his face.

"King Fernholz has lost his wart," she echoed.

"Yes."

She stepped forward then, reached her hand up and touched Clemmy's face. His heart raced with pleasure at her gentle touch.

"And you have gained a wart," she said softly.

"I . . . I have?"

"I'm sure it wasn't there before," Libby said.

Clemmy felt the wart. She was telling the truth. It was very curious. He decided he would think about it later.

"Will you marry the King?" he blurted out. Libby seemed to grow very sad at his question. She shook her head.

"You won't? But why?"

She sighed and stared at the floor. "Because . . ."

"Because what?"

"Because." She stalled for a moment and then looked Clemmy squarely in the eye. "Because he has freckles," she said.

"Oh no," Clemmy said.

"Yes," she insisted. "He is terribly freckled and I could never marry a man with so many freckles! I'm sorry."

Clemmy was frustrated to the point of anger. He turned and looked across the green lawns. He felt he had lived this moment before, that very day.

"And if King Fernholz had no freckles, Lady Libby, then would you marry him?"

She considered his question for a moment before

answering. "When King Fernholz is clear skinned, then you may come and ask me again," she said. She smiled at Clemmy and pushed the door shut.

Never in his life had Clemmy felt so many contradictory emotions at one time. As he walked slowly away from the stubborn Libby's house, he thought of her soft hand touching his cheek (his wart!) and felt a warm and excited rush. No village girl was ever like the beautiful Libby. And he asked himself what possible difference it could make even if she accepted Fernholz' proposal, with acres and acres of Turks sharpening their blades. He crossed the green lawns and he thought and he thought.

King Fernholz was in love. That part was easy to understand. And the King wanted sons. These were proper matters for a king, Clemmy thought. Also, Fernholz' romantic problems posed less danger than the Turk, and yet the King claimed to be dying of despair, as if the Lady Libby held his very life in her hands!

So, Clemmy thought, hmmmm. So what? And then, with a sinking feeling in his stomach, he came to a frightening realization. He realized, there under the great leafy trees, that he also had to save Fernholz from the Turk! Or die trying. A shudder of fear ran through him, and he leaned against one of the old trees. He felt the ridiculous wart on his face and wondered if he was going mad. The wart, he reasoned, he must have got from touching

Shiefelbine's toady old bag.

At last he took a deep breath and spoke to the air, to the path, to the trees.

"I'll do it! I swear I'll do it. There's no turning back now."

As he crossed the deserted marketplace, he heard his name called out by the unmistakable deep voice of Magnus the shepherd, who had gotten him into this mess. The huge man approached him wearing his simple peasant clothes. He smelled of sheep.

"Hello, Clemmy. How is the reading going?"

"Magnus! You must know the Turk is on our doorstep," Clemmy said quickly.

"Aye. I had just brought in a hundred yearling ewes to the stable when the doorman slammed the city gates shut. I guess we were too late," he said sadly. "Maybe things would have been different if I had found you sooner." Clemmy heard the sound of defeat in his voice.

"No," Clemmy said, "I think you were only just in time." He probably sounded more hopeful than he felt, but the big friendly man helped shore up his courage.

"Magnus, we have to go and talk to the Turk," he said, not knowing where the words came from.

"We . . . ?" Magnus sounded doubtful. And worried.

"Yes. We. You and I together. Wearing your helmet and sword, and riding on the warhorse."

"It's not really a warhorse. Am I to fight all those thousands of Turks?"

"We'll just talk to them. You know, explain things. Beg for peace. Make a deal with them. We can't fight them."

"The Turk didn't come all this way for an explanation." Magnus laughed. "They will probably kill us."

"But if we do nothing, they will smash open the gates and kill us anyway." This depressing logic sounded to Magnus like: You can die now or you can die later. It was not very persuasive.

"Well, anyway, I'm going," said Clemmy. "If you want to come along, meet me by the gates in an hour."

Clemmy walked purposefully away. Magnus watched him disappear. He studied his own long shadow. The afternoon had slipped away. Soon it would be nightfall.

Armor

Clemmy found Fernholz eating mutton happily in the dining chamber. When he entered, the King leaped to his feet and rushed toward Clemmy. His chair tumbled over backward. His crown was askew, and his robe flew like a cape behind him. The aroma of the food filled Clemmy's nostrils.

"Well? What took you so long? Am I engaged to the Lady? What did she say? Out with it! Speak, lad!" He gripped Clemmy's shoulders in his long arms and stared close into his face. All Clemmy could see was freckles.

"Freckles," he said. It was the first word that came to his mind.

"Freckles, yes! Freckles. What?"

"We've got to get rid of them," Clemmy said quickly. He wished that Fernholz would let loose of him. The King's expression clouded in bewilderment.

"She won't marry a man with freckles," Clemmy explained. "She feels very strongly about it."

"She won't marry me? Because of my freckles?" Fernholz was incredulous. And exasperated. And disappointed. And then devastated. He let go of Clemmy and clasped his hands to his face. Then he sank into a chair and stared blankly. His whole body seemed to shake with stunned surprise, as if he had been struck a blow. It was not mere discouragement Clemmy saw but vanished hopes, murdered hopes. The grandeur of the King's suffering made Clemmy's stomach tighten. King Fernholz had no armor to protect himself against the Lady's rejection.

"She liked the bit with the wart, sir. I think you should let me try again," Clemmy said. "Maybe we can have a go at the freckles."

"Yes," the King said absently, only vaguely hearing. And then the words sank in, and he turned his forlorn gaze on Clemmy. "Yes. Yes! Of course! You must help me. God has guided you here, surely."

"God has guided others here as well," Clemmy said quietly.

"Ahhh!" Fernholz shook his head and waved his arm in the air, as if swatting at a fly. Clemmy was amazed. He helped himself to half a loaf of bread from the King's table and headed for the garden.

There he found the old man Shiefelbine very much alive and even awake. He was sitting among the many colored flowers in his shabby old wedding

robe, taking long sniffs. Clemmy watched him become very still and then turn toward Clemmy, standing quietly thirty paces away. Shiefelbine crinkled
his face into a smile, stood and shuffled back toward
his bench.

"They said you were here, and so you are," he
croaked.

"Who said?" Clemmy asked.

"The flowers, of course. Many flowers tell lies. It's
a nasty habit they learned from the insects. You
have to be careful whom you believe nowadays."

Clemmy didn't know what to say. The old man
had perceptions that confounded belief, but it
seemed impossible to ask him about it, to start at the
beginning. Not only did he talk to plants but he
didn't believe them! If flowers could talk, why would
they talk to him? And why would they lie? If you
had to live your entire life in a cave to know these
things, eating toads, sleeping on damp rocks, was it
worth it? Shiefelbine left him speechless.

"You've come to pray again, from the book,
haven't you? Yes? Well, it's a fine day for prayers,"
he said. "I feel like a young man again. I think I
may live another hundred years!"

Live another hundred years! You may be cut in
half by the Turk before bedtime, Clemmy thought.
Shiefelbine sat down on the bench.

"The King's wart is gone. Now we are trying to
remove his spots."

"His spots? The King has spots?"

"Freckles, sir. Is there such a prayer in the book?"

Shiefelbine frowned. "Is it for a good reason, removing the spots? You remember, boy, these are imperfect prayers. God made heaven and earth—do you think he can't handle a few freckles? But I wouldn't trifle with Him!" He wagged a finger at Clemmy. "Why should we bother the Almighty about freckles?"

"For love, sir."

"For love! Yes. Well. Fetch the bag!"

Clemmy didn't want to touch the bag again. "It's there, by your feet, sir."

"Well, get out our book, lad."

In the dusty quartermaster's closet, Magnus found the armor, the breastplate and sword and the uncomfortable helmet (it was too small for him) where he had put them only that morning. He hadn't expected to be taking them out again.

Sighing heavily, he gathered these military vestments and laid them on a bench. It would have pleased him more to slip away, to return to the high pastures where his own family lived and tended the flocks. He had been called to serve the King because of his great size, but just then he was feeling rather small. One man against a host of genuine soldiers who had been trained to take lives, not tend sheep.

The odds were piled up on the side of the Turk.

It would not have inspired Magnus' confidence to know that in the palace garden, Clemmy was praying to remove the King's freckles.

Sana me, Domine, quoniam conturbata sunt ossa mea . . .
SANA ME, DOMINE, QUONIAM CONTURBATA SUNT OSSA MEA!

Rugio propter fremitum cordis mei . . .
RUGIO PROPTER FREMITUM CORDIS MEI!

Magnus slipped the heavy breastplate around him and fastened it tight. He thought of sheep butchering. It was never a pleasant job, of course, but a necessary part of being a herdsman. Magnus liked sheep, and he thought of how he always said he was sorry before he killed a sheep. He ate the meat with respect and thanksgiving. Magnus' mother had taught him to offer thanks for their daily food, for good weather, green pastures and healthy animals.

Viribus morbi domitis, saluti restituuntur . . .
VIRIBUS MORBI DOMITIS, SALUTI RESTI-TUUNTUR!

Et oratio fidei salvabit infirmum . . .
ET ORATIO FIDEI SALVABIT INFIRMUM!

The sword hung from his hip like a dead branch on a great tree. With an effort he squeezed his large head into the leather helmet and fastened the strap beneath his bearded chin. Will I be given a burial or be left to rot on the ground to be eaten by birds? Why should I do this mad thing? Because it would be cowardice to let Clemmy go alone, he answered himself, and walked heavily out the door.

Outnumbered

C lemmy was relieved to find Magnus waiting for him at the city gates. The great oaken doors were shut, fortunately, but Clemmy saw no sign of the doorman.

"I wouldn't go out there if I were you," Marbelard cautioned from his perch atop the wall.

"Where is the gatekeeper?" Magnus called up.

"Gone. He gave me his ring!" Marbelard smiled and climbed down. The new doorman bowed gracefully (more or less) and then stood, almost straight, weaving in his own way. His humped shoulder bobbed and his tilted face smiled up at Magnus on the horse. And then he looked at Clemmy.

"You've got the pox," Marbelard said.

"The pox?" Clemmy asked in surprise. "No I don't."

"You've got spots! Like the King."

Clemmy looked at his arms. It was true! He wet his hand with his tongue and rubbed, but there was no mistaking it. Freckles. All over him. A moment of confusion came and went. He realized finally what was happening. Shiefelbine's imperfect prayers were transferring King Fernholz' afflictions to him! First the wart and now the freckles!

As always in Mulberia, there was never enough time to think about things. Clemmy searched his friends' faces, then looked at the horse, the dirt, the city gates. He looked for something, anything, an answer. He opened his mouth, but no words came out. He had never in his whole life been so amazed. A thousand thoughts rushed into his brain at once.

Shiefelbine's dog-eared *En Supplico Mirabilis* was a miracle book after all. And without a doubt, King Fernholz was now completely unfreckled and dancing in front of his looking glass. Clemmy was happy to have succeeded in this, for the King's sake. Surely the Lady Libby could not refuse him now. His mind lingered on his memory of her lovely face. Ah yes, he recalled her very words. She could never marry a man with so many freckles.

"Open the gates, now, please," Magnus said, breaking the spell.

Marbelard frowned. "They've got you outnumbered, Sir Magnus," he said.

As they passed between the wide wooden doors, Marbelard bowed in farewell. His words echoed in Clemmy's mind. Outnumbered. Outnumbered. Yes, he thought, they have us outnumbered. But they don't know that, do they?

The Charge

From Marbelard's vantage point high on the wall, even large Magnus on horseback seemed diminished crossing the half mile that separated the city walls and the wide ranks of Turkish cavalry. The Turks had formed into battle lines that stretched as wide and as far as he could see. The sun had at last begun its descent behind the peaks on the western horizon. If there was to be an assault on Mulberia, Marbelard thought, it would have to proceed by torchlight.

On the other hand, he mused, the Turkish horde could probably have supper, do their chores, take a nap, have an evening prayer service and still conquer the city before the stars came out.

In fact, a detail of the Sultan's potato peelers armed with pots and pans would have been enough to conquer the undefended city.

Watching Clemmy and Magnus growing smaller on the horizon, Marbelard's stomach churned with hopeless dread. And then he began to hear the drumming.

Clemmy walked slowly in front of Magnus and Birch, the would-be warhorse. As the gap narrowed between them and the first rank of Turks, Clemmy allowed himself only one backward glance. He saw the tiny figure of Marbelard on the wall and he saw the towers of King Fernholz' palace. Magnus rode silently, looking as fierce as he could manage under the circumstances. Birch was jittery and nervous, smelling the many horses that stretched in lines before them. And then Clemmy heard the drumming.

The Turks began beating their shields with the hilts of their swords. It began softly and then was taken up by the thousands of warriors. The metallic staccato beat swept over Clemmy and Magnus like a wave of doom, echoing off the city walls behind them. Magnus reined his mount hard to keep the frightened horse from bolting away.

Clemmy halted in fear. The drumming stopped, not at once but slowly, as if a signal was passed from front to back. And then there was a terrible silence. Clemmy began walking forward again, and the rhythm of sword on shield resumed, matching his stride: step *KLACK!*, step *KLACK!*, step *K-KLAACK-KK!*

They were close enough to clearly see the dark-skinned Turks sitting boldly in their saddles. They could see the brightly colored silk clothing, plumed red hats and brocaded battle flags. The horses' livery gleamed with silver, which flashed in the setting sun.

Barely two hundred yards separated them when the Turks added their voices to the drumming. A single fierce high-pitched howl was joined by a second voice and then a third, and was then taken up by the multitude. A virtual wall of sound roared across the shepherds' plain and swept over the city walls. The roar went through the cracks, around the corners and into every mouse hole of Mulberia. High on his ledge, misshapen Marbelard burst into tears.

Clemmy halted again, involuntarily, awash in the deafening Turkish bray. A shudder ran the length of him and he was frozen in his reluctant dutiful tracks.

And then, as if the drumming and horrible clamor weren't frightening enough, suddenly a single mounted Turk broke from the line and charged at them, swinging his blade, shrieking like a wild man. Clemmy's eyes were fixed on the galloping Turk who would cross the short distance in less than ten seconds. Behind Clemmy, Magnus drew his own borrowed sword, held it aloft and dug his heels hard into Birch's flanks. His obedient horse leaped forward past Clemmy and, with head down and ears back, charged toward the oncoming Turk. Magnus' huge voice roared out like a roll of thunder. The two horsemen charged toward each other, hoofs pounding and steel flashing in the air.

On the Carpet

Magnus and the Turk flew at one another and the crescendo of Turkish voices reached a deafening peak. The charging horses churned the dusty ground into two brown swirling storms behind them. Clemmy lowered his head and closed his eyes, not wanting to see the inevitable worst. And then it was over. The roaring voices receded like the wind dying after a gale.

When the two warriors were no more than thirty yards apart, the Turk reined his horse hard to a stop. The dust caught up and swirled about him. Magnus, intent on survival, saw the Arabian warhorse dig in and rear on its hind legs. And so he did the same. Birch pitched abruptly to a stop, not as gracefully as his well-trained counterpart. Magnus hung on to avoid being thrown, and suddenly both riders were at a standstill. Their nervous horses snorted for air and pawed the ground.

Clemmy opened his eyes at last to see the Turk

warrior sheathing his sword and walking his fine black horse toward Magnus. Birch began to back up, but Magnus held him fast and the two men studied each other's faces. The Turk was dark eyed and had a mustache. When he stopped again, only a dozen feet away, he smiled at Magnus and arched one eyebrow. There is nothing funny about this, Magnus thought grimly, and frowned at the Turk, holding his own sword at the ready.

Finally the Turkish soldier spoke loudly, words that Magnus didn't understand. It sounded bossy and not at all friendly. The man was wearing leather leggings and a wide, shimmering, dark-blue sash across his middle. His long robelike shirt was a lighter shade of blue with wide sleeves, fastened with gold buttons. A red-and-white embroidered cape was attached at the shoulders and billowed behind him in the afternoon breeze.

If it had been only a fashion show, the Turk would have beaten Magnus hands down. Magnus, in his sweaty woolens, squeezed into his drab gray breastplate and capped with the too-tight leather helmet, was getting a terrible headache. He hazarded a glance back toward Clemmy.

Clemmy came forward and stopped beside Magnus, looking at the colorful, frightening Turk at close range. Giving up on tight-lipped Magnus, the man turned his attention to Clemmy. He spoke a few words very forcefully and then pointed at both of them and gestured over his shoulder to the army behind him. Then, turning his mount, he set off at a trot.

Magnus and Clemmy exchanged a glance of uncertainty, and then Clemmy walked after the horseman. Magnus spoke softly to Birch and nudged him forward with his heels.

As they neared the line of cavalry, the Turks made an opening. A narrow path between the thousands appeared. Clemmy entered into this gauntlet without visible hesitation. Magnus rode behind him, and the opening in the equestrian sea closed behind them. Magnus had the feeling of being swallowed up. He tried not to look to either side. It was most difficult.

Clemmy had recovered from the paralyzing fear of the moment just past. He felt almost dizzy with relief at not being killed already.

As he walked, he looked upward at the faces of the Turk riders who lined the narrow way. Their bright vests and jeweled shirts showed they were very proud in conducting war. Most wore turbans, and almost every one, Clemmy noticed, wore a carefully groomed black mustache. This solidarity spared them the necessity of being individual thoughtful men, and yet, as Clemmy looked at their dark and handsome faces, he read many different emotions in their eyes.

Some lifted their mustaches with cruel or condescending smiles and some frowned with distrust. There were some who would not return his gaze or who looked away nervously. And there were many who were clearly afraid, fixing their dark and worried eyes upon him, Clemmy, the enemy. Of course, the sight of Magnus gave them little comfort. He was easily a head taller than the largest Turk on the field.

When they emerged from the last ranks of the great army, they saw a hundred wagons heavy with supplies or items looted from destroyed villages. Central among the wagons was a fine blue-and-white silk tent that billowed lightly in the breeze. Many armed men stood around the tent. Carpets and tables had been arranged in front. A group of older men stood by the tables.

The Turkish horseman whom Clemmy and Magnus had followed through the multitude dismounted and handed the reins of his horse to another man. He gestured at Magnus to do the same.

They followed the Turk on foot toward the tent, and as they stepped onto the soft braided carpet, the Turk bowed formally to those who stood before him. All eyes turned to Clemmy and Magnus. Magnus had a feeling of dread tumbling about in his stomach, and inside his impromptu war outfit he was running with sweat.

A graybeard Turk with a white turban and yellow-and-white robes drew Clemmy and Magnus closer with a curled finger. He had a curved dagger at his side under a deep-red sash that circled his waist. The man had a careful and commanding appearance.

Clemmy placed his feet apart and hands on hips in an effort to appear businesslike and unafraid. He saw the sun dipping quickly toward the jagged western horizon.

The old Turk, with another finger gesture, drew a man from the group toward him and spoke to him. The voice Clemmy heard was measured and inquisitive. The second Turk turned and spoke to Clemmy.

"What have you brought?" he said sharply.

Clemmy couldn't believe his ears! It was the second time that day he had been asked that question.

"Hah!" he said loudly, surprising himself. "I have brought something. Do you know what it is that I have brought?"

Suleiman the Magnificent

The Turkish interpreter (who knew seven languages) raised his brows and cocked his head to make sure he had heard correctly. He then chattered sidelong to his master. The old Turk listened, never taking his eyes off Clemmy. He answered with a long sentence.

"He says you have brought a clumsy horse and a stinking giant. He wants to know if you speak for the King of this city."

"I have brought you hope!" Clemmy said loudly, and he pointed his finger at the old Turk. More chatter.

"I have brought you one chance to save yourself! A warning, sir." The interpreter blanched at Clemmy's words and then translated them. Clemmy pointed at the glorious golden sunset.

"Tomorrow the sun will set on no living Turk on this field. Go back the way you came! Or die." His voice became a rasping growl. His face had contorted into an angry mask. His eyes bored into the leader's face. Beside Clemmy, trying to look fierce, Magnus made a soft high-pitched noise. It was an involuntary sound of astonishment, heard only by Clemmy. The interpreter spoke a long time to the Turkish chieftain. He also pointed toward the setting sun.

The Turk turned then with some uncertainty and looked over his shoulder toward the tent. He looked back at Clemmy and Magnus, shuffled his old feet and bit his lower lip. Of course he was not the Sultan, Clemmy realized.

He was, in fact, the grand vizier, Ibrahim Pasha, a Greek man who was the Sultan's governor, diplomat and commander of his army.

Ibrahim Pasha was a very capable man. He was, Clemmy thought, considering getting another opinion.

"My King wants to know"—Clemmy spoke again, pausing for the interpreter—"what are your burial customs?" He turned and made a sweeping gesture with his hand toward the great mass of the Turkish army. "It's going to be a very big job."

His words were passed on to the Turkish governor, who began to look unsure of himself. He spoke a few short words to the other man, turned and disappeared into the fine tent. Magnus let out a long hissing breath, which he had been holding inside.

Ibrahim Pasha reappeared after a few interminable minutes and called to the interpreter.

"He says you come inside," the man said, leading the way. A young boy pulled back the wide silk flap over the entrance. Clemmy nudged Magnus forward. His huge friend had to stoop to enter.

Inside, lanterns were lit and several more boys stood ready to serve the Sultan. As his eyes adjusted to the light, Clemmy was surprised to hear birdsong, and to smell the perfume of fresh flowers. And there, standing opposite the doorway with his back toward Clemmy, was the great Turk, Suleiman the Magnificent. He poured water from a jeweled pitcher into glass vases of flowers. On either side stood large bird-cages with dozens of tiny colorful birds on wooden perches.

Suleiman the Magnificent turned at last to his guests. His robes were gold and black, tied off with a red-and-orange embroidered cloth that had a swirling pattern of diamonds sewn into it. He wore a perfectly white turban with an enormous black jewel attached to the front. He was more colorful than either the flowers or the birds.

Clemmy was surprised to find him much younger than the grand vizier. He was tall and thin, long necked and curve nosed. He too wore a black mustache. He had a long face, and his dark eyes showed fearlessness. He appraised first Clemmy and then Magnus in silence. Finally he spoke. His voice was grave.

"Suleiman the Magnificent asks what is the size

of your King's army, which dares to make threats?" said the interpreter.

"Fernholz the Wolf," Clemmy shot back fiercely, "bids you leave before you feel his terrible jaws." Clemmy bared his teeth. The Sultan had no visible reaction to this gesture or to the jumble of words that poured from the interpreter.

"Fernholz the Wolf," Suleiman repeated the King's new nickname. Again he spoke evenly to the interpreter.

"Suleiman the Magnificent has never heard of this wolf. How many men does he command?"

"None have lived to repeat his name who came waving swords and bleating like sheep in his pasture," Clemmy answered. "The wolf hungers for the sheep! Tomorrow he will feed." He opened his eyes wide, making a face at the Turk, and then he licked his lips with relish. He spoke again.

"He has in his garden a red pond that is filled with the blood of his enemies," Clemmy paused. "He has a hundred trunks that are filled with their teeth."

Suleiman listened to Clemmy's boasts with some surprise. No one had ever spoken to him like this before. He had never suffered a military defeat. Most small kingdoms that appeared on his path threw down arms and begged for terms. His ships controlled the Mediterranean Sea and his empire reached from Algiers to Bucharest, from Budapest to Constantinople. He spoke in his own tongue for several minutes with the vizier Ibrahim Pasha. Magnus longed to be away.

At last Suleiman nodded toward the Turk who served as translator, and the man said, "You do not answer the question which you are twice being asked. How many men does your King command?"

"How many snakes live in the rocks?" Clemmy pulled back his sleeve and slowly reached his hand forward. When his arm was fully extended and all eyes were upon it, he jerked his hand back in mock terror. "Put your hand in and find out!" This time even Suleiman the Magnificent was startled by Clemmy's forcefulness. Clemmy judged that his opportunity in diplomacy was nearly over, one way or another. He pointed away to the south.

"Go! And live! Or stay and die," he growled. "I have no more to say to you. The King awaits our return."

Suleiman raised a hand after hearing Clemmy's final words. A small smile played across his lips and then vanished. With the palm of his hand he gestured toward Clemmy and then toward the door flap. He spoke again. His voice was controlled, even courteous.

"Suleiman the Magnificent will order his many men to make camp for this night. He will consider your words and he will pray to Allah for guidance. And now you may go."

Clemmy and Magnus exchanged a quick glance

and were about to turn away when Suleiman spoke again and gestured with his hand toward Magnus.

"And you may stay," the interpreter said to Magnus. Suleiman watched Magnus' face cloud with confusion. He turned to Clemmy in panic and said simply, "What?"

The Sultan spoke again, and then came the words they could understand.

"Suleiman must insist that you accept his hospitality," the man said. "You will stay here tonight."

"I'm going with him!" Magnus exclaimed, indicating Clemmy. Suleiman was watching Magnus closely. "We go together. I don't care for your hospitality and I'm going!"

A dozen Turks, the Sultan's private guards, entered the tent and stood in a line, hands on hips, each with a short curved sword ready at his waist. Looking around the guards, the interpreter spoke to Clemmy.

"He stays. You go. Back to your wolf. There is no argument."

Magnus' hand gripped Clemmy's arm in fear as the tent flap was pulled back by one of the boys. A damp, cool breeze swept across them.

Clemmy looked into Magnus' frightened face. He saw beads of sweat hanging on his great forehead, and there was a tremble in his powerful hand. Clemmy's heart clenched with awful guilt. Magnus had never wanted to come in the first place, and he,

Clemmy, had shamed him into it. Was the Sultan planning to torture Magnus? Clemmy couldn't endure the thought.

"Why must he stay?" he protested loudly.

"It is the will of Suleiman. Go now!"

Magnus relaxed his grip on Clemmy's arm. His eyes swept across the faces of the Sultan's guards. Though not as big as he, they were muscular and unafraid. He couldn't fight them, and running away was out of the question. Best to do nothing until Clemmy was away.

He leaned down to Clemmy at last and whispered, "Don't come back." And then with one huge hand he pushed him gently toward the doorway. With great reluctance, Clemmy left the tent and walked, head down, through the wretched restless horde and back to the city of Mulberia.

After Clemmy was gone, Suleiman brightened, even smiled at Magnus and offered him a canvas chair. The Sultan sat opposite him, flanked by the sturdy guards. Suleiman leaned back comfortably and wove his long fingers together, looking very pleased with himself. He spoke cheerfully.

Magnus thought of his mother at home in the high pastures. He brought her large happy face into focus and heard her laughter. In his mind she called his name. Magnus! . . . Maaaaagnusss! Come in now!

"Suleiman the Magnificent says now we will talk about the wolf king."

A Wonderful Wife

With the disappearance of the sun the long shadows erased themselves and twilight gathered around the small and dejected figure who returned alone to the city gates. Marbelard, high on the wall, watched Clemmy approach. His eyes reached also for Magnus, strained for Magnus, swept the darkening horizon for Magnus. But no matter how hard he looked, there was no Magnus.

Clemmy crossed the King's pasture and slipped through Marbelard's great creaking door. They did not speak until the door was shut and bolted. Marbelard's emotions were as jumbled as his appearance. His unfocussing gaze fell one way on Clemmy's tired face and another way toward nothing at all, empty space—no Magnus.

His question hung in the air, too raw to be spoken. Clemmy leaned heavily against the door.

"Magnus was not hurt," he said. "Not when I left him, anyway. The Turk forced him to stay behind."

He shook his head with remorse. Marbelard stood perfectly still in the semidarkness, and once more tears came to his eyes. He reached out and touched Clemmy with his good hand, and the two young men embraced in their sorrow.

At last Marbelard gathered his strength and released his friend. He elected not to speak of Magnus.

"So tomorrow there will be war?" he asked.

"Yes," Clemmy answered. "A very short war when you consider that our entire army has already been captured. Marbelard . . ."

"What?"

"You could take some food and slip away, through the doors, tonight."

"I won't do it!" Marbelard seemed shocked by the very idea. "I'm staying with you!"

Loyalty can carry a high price, Clemmy thought. Loyalty to a friend or loyalty to a king, why should these things be so dangerous?

"If you last through tomorrow, Marbelard, I predict you will live a long and happy life." It was the best he could do.

Leaving the lonely wall, they found their way to the King's larder, the palace pantry. And there, like two petty thieves, they ate freely of the few loaves of hardening bread. They cut large wedges from the royal cheese and drained a flask of Fernholz' wine. Although nothing was changed, it cheered them to eat. A few less morsels for Suleiman the bloody

Magnificent, Clemmy thought.

"Marbelard, I want you to do me two favors," he said. Marbelard grunted affirmatively, his mouth full of bread.

"Go and speak with the King. Tell him that I've gone again to see the Lady Libby with news about his departed freckles. Please make no mention of my own." He smiled in spite of himself. There was something absurdly funny about Shiefelbine's incompetent prayers and the migrating freckles. Not to mention the wart.

"I will do it," Marbelard bobbed his head.

"Also, I want you to go and visit my mother. Just make sure she's comfortable. And . . ."

"I will tell her that you love her very much!"

"Well, yes. Keep her company. Show her your fine ring," Clemmy said. He began to load food into a wicker basket. He found potatoes and onions and a small cabbage. To these he added a dry slab of mutton and some bread. What have you brought? he said to himself. And then he turned again to Marbelard.

"When the sun is up, even before the dew is off the grass, I'm going back to get Magnus," he said seriously. "I'll meet you by the city gates at that hour. And now I must go."

"I will be there!" Marbelard promised emphatically, and made something like a salute.

Clemmy retraced his steps in the darkness

through the market, between the trees and across the lawns, and for a third time he stood at Libby's front door. The lamps were lit inside. Clemmy knocked on the Lady's door. He knocked again.

At last a voice, Aunt Lucia's, called from behind the unmoving door. "Who is it? What do you want?"

Clemmy imagined fifty of the flamboyant mustached Turks in his place on the doorstep, pounding on the door, having to deal with the stalwart auntie.

"It is I! Clemmy. I've brought you some food!"

"Leave it there," she shouted. "Go away!"

He sighed. With a tired laugh in his voice, he called back, "I will not go away! Don't be silly. Open up!"

To his surprise, she did just that. The door swung open slowly, revealing Aunt Lucia peeking, and then opened enough for her two arms to reach for Clemmy's basket. He placed it in her hands and spoke before she could slam the door.

"Please. A word with the Lady Libby. A message from the King. I'll only stay a moment."

"Wait here," she said wearily. It seemed almost too easy, Clemmy thought. The food basket had worked.

He stepped into the shadowy entry. A slender candle burned on a wall fixture and provided the only direct light in the passage. Beyond the half-open door to the sitting room he saw a corner of that room bathed in the warm light of oil lamps. Clemmy blew out the hallway candle.

He was in the dark hallway then when Aunt Lucia returned, followed by Libby. They halted in the parlor doorway.

"Dear Aunt, please," Clemmy said, "may we speak privately? It's terribly important."

"Certainly not!" the aunt returned briskly.

Libby spoke a word into her aunt's ear. Lucia harumphed and went through a side door to the kitchen. And then, as the beautiful Libby smiled at Clemmy in the half-light, all the thoughts in his head vanished, gone like dry leaves in an autumn wind.

"Hello, Clemmy," she said softly. "Will you come into the parlor?"

"Umm . . . no, I only came to tell you about the King's freckles," he said, turning his face away from the lamplight.

"The King's freckles?" Libby was surprised and amused. "Well, what is it you want to tell me about them, the freckles?"

Clemmy laughed out loud. It was a ridiculous thing to talk about, especially under the circumstances of impending war. "They're gone. Removed. Vanished. Through devout prayers. Again King Fernholz begs you to consider him worthy of marriage." He leaned against the wall wearily.

Clemmy's news failed to produce the desired effect. Libby pursed her lips and tilted her lovely face to one side, thinking. First the wart and now the freckles. She tried to picture the King's face without them. In her mind, Fernholz' face wore a worried grin, a nervous hopefulness, sincerity but not wisdom. She tried with some difficulty to picture the King praying, and yet he had succeeded in his selfish misguided prayers. Could it be, Libby wondered, that heaven is as disorganized as the kingdom of Mulberia? No! It could not be! She could not marry the man, no matter his love or his prayers.

"You did say, Lady Libby, that it was the freckles and the wart that put you off the King," Clemmy reminded her.

"Yes. Yes I did, but . . ."

"But?"

In the shadowy hallway, Clemmy stared at her, speechless. He no longer cared whether she would marry King Fernholz. It seemed a matter of no importance. And yet he knew that the King would be shattered again by her refusal.

"What fault is it, then, that remains in the King? In all fairness, don't you think you should tell him once and for all?"

"Yes. Yes I do. You're absolutely right," she said.

"What shall I tell him, then?" Clemmy said, knowing already what her answer would be.

"You think I've been inventing excuses."

"Yes." Clemmy smiled unseen.

"You want to know the absolute truth about why

I will not accept his proposal? It's not easy refusing such an emotional King. I don't enjoy hurting people's feelings."

"No, of course not. I understand completely. I really do."

"You do?"

"Yes, although, forgive me, I do think you would make a wonderful wife and queen." Clemmy blushed, filling in the empty space around his new freckles. His weariness left him as his own affections were given voice. "But please, may I give him your reason?"

"The reason?"

"Yes. "

"It is . . ." She hesitated.

"Go ahead."

"It's his limp! I'm sorry, but I could never marry a man with such a limp." Libby wrung her hands together and watched Clemmy nod knowingly. He took one last look at her in the half-light and stepped away, through the door. She followed, stopping at the threshold.

"What will happen tomorrow, Clemmy?" she asked.

"God will decide," he answered. "It will be a day to remember," he added hopefully, and strode away into the starlight.

A Little Smile

E ven in a strange story such as this, what happened next was quite predictable. The only surprise was the unaccountable wisp of a smile that returned again and again to Clemmy's lips. The excitable King, minus freckles, overlooked the phantom smile as his marriage hopes crumbled once more. He overlooked it again as he pondered his wretched lame foot. Clemmy slipped quietly away to his mother's room and left a soft kiss on her pale sleeping cheek.

Clemmy said nothing about Magnus to King Fernholz. Nor did he speak of the Turk. Did Suleiman the Magnificent speak that night of King Fernholz? Fernholz the Wolf? All around the world, Clemmy rightly assumed, warrior kings spoke of their enemies as they sharpened their blades, plotted death, and prayed for glorious, blood-washed victories. Only here, in misbegotten Mulberia was a king foolish enough to be dying of love, praying to be worthy of a beautiful young woman who worried about sparing the King's feelings on this, the night before his certain death. It was thoughts such as these that brought the small and hidden smile to Clemmy's lips.

Before taking to his own bed, he resolved to once more guide Shiefelbine's prayers in the morning. If the King must die, he thought, then let him die standing straight and with renewed hopes. But it was very, very late. He closed his eyes and let the night take him.

The First Casualty of War

"Wake up!" Clemmy whispered, shaking Shiefelbine by the shoulders. The old man slept on the ground beside his bench, next to the pond. He resisted waking, opening one old eye only and, sensing (not seeing) the pale predawn light, closed it. Clemmy shook him again.

"It's me. Clemmy. Wake up, please. We must pray again. To save the King."

Shiefelbine stirred finally and crawled on all fours to the edge of the pond. He splashed water on his ancient wrinkled face and yawned. The old man guided Clemmy to the proper page in the prayer book, and Clemmy read over the Latin words.

"This morning, I want you to memorize the last line of the prayer before we start," Clemmy said. "And then don't speak it until I am well away. Do you agree?" It was his own leg he was worried about. If proximity had anything to do with it, it was worth trying to avoid taking on Fernholz' limp.

And so in the growing light of dawn Clemmy read the words in *En Supplico Mirabilis*. Shiefelbine flung them loudly toward heaven until they reached the last line. Clemmy patted him on the back and dashed away, around the palace and toward the city gate.

High on his ledge, Marbelard was already standing, waiting for Clemmy. On top of the wall he had placed twelve spoons in a row, their business ends toward the glow of the Turkish fires across the sheep-shearing plain. These spoons Marbelard had discovered in Jude's room the night before. The old woman had stolen them from the King's pantry!

Back on the ground he pulled the gates open so that Clemmy could slip out.

"They are mounting their horses and forming into lines again," Marbelard said fearfully, weaving from side to side in the growing dawn light. It was terrible news.

"Don't be afraid, Marbelard," Clemmy said, squeezing his friend's arm. "We will have a fine breakfast when Magnus and I return." Clemmy gave a wink and then turned away. He went through the doors quickly. As he walked away, he heard the hinges creak behind him.

In the King's garden, Shiefelbine stood stiffly on his bench, holding *The Book of Marvelous Prayers* to his chest. He held his head cocked, as if listening. Perhaps he heard Marbelard dropping the heavy wooden bolt across the city gates.

Clemmy strode toward the Turkish battle lines which he could see clearly in the dawn light. His nostrils filled with the smoke from their fires. The morning air was cool, and he pulled the hood of his cloak over his head. He hadn't gone more than a hundred yards when the Turks began their drumming for a second time. The *klack* of sword on shield kept time with Clemmy's deliberate pace across the plain. The noise reached over the city walls and into the King's garden. Shiefelbine's shaggy head nodded in time with the beat.

And then, according to his destiny, Shiefelbine shouted out the last line of the prayer to save the King and followed it with a great echoing *AMEN!* Having done this, the ragged old miracle man had used up his lifetime allotment of words. He slowly stepped down from the bench and returned *En Supplico Mirabilis* to his tattered bag. He then sat on the bench, leaned his head back and died.

Royal Dreams

The ground passed slowly under Clemmy's feet. His hide boots dampened with the morning dew. The hypnotic drumming of the Turk dulled his senses. His eyes were fixed on the ground before him. Step *KLACK*, step *KLACK*. The empty space between Clemmy and the Turk narrowed.

And then, not noticeably at first, the cadence changed. Absorbed in his thoughts, Clemmy paid no attention to the stiffness that overtook his left leg. It was not painful, but slowly he lost the knee's flexibility and then he began to drag the foot. The Turkish drummers beat twice, paused, and then beat twice again. Clemmy noticed the drums' change even before he became aware of his new limp, the King's limp.

King Fernholz himself, with his miraculously healed leg, was still snoring in the royal bedchamber. He had not awakened when Shiefelbine stood shouting from the bench in the garden. Nor had he awakened when the multitude of Turks began their drumming. The royal dreams were unassailable.

Clemmy felt himself grow clumsy, dragging his stiff leg. He nearly fell down twice but slowed his pace and hobbled onward. It was upsetting to become suddenly crippled, even for a good cause. He thought of Marbelard's deformities, which were far worse than his own. And he thought of the Lady Libby, who could never marry a man so terribly freckled with a wart and a limp.

These were brief thoughts, each passing quickly. As he neared the Turkish lines, he focussed his eyes on the horsemen and thought of Magnus. How long, he wondered, did his giant friend resist the Sultan's torture before crying out the truth about Mulberia? And then did they kill him? He heard Magnus' words in his mind: Don't come back.

A high-pitched shout came from one of the horsemen and the drumming ceased. As they had done the day before, the Turks opened a path through the middle of their ranks. Their impatient horses snorted and pawed the ground with their hoofs. This time Clemmy looked neither left nor right as he passed among them.

When he emerged from the narrow path between the thousands of Turkish soldiers, he saw again the Sultan's gaily colored tent. He was met by the same graybeard Turk and the nervous interpreter. For a long moment they stood face-to-face, each waiting for the other to speak first.

"Aren't you going to ask me what I brought?" Clemmy asked with bitterness in his voice. His odd question was repeated to the old Turk, who answered, pointing his finger to the east.

"Ibrahim Pasha says you brought the sun." The grand vizier spoke again. "And now, he says, it is time for you to die for the glory of Allah!"

Behind him, Clemmy heard many blades pulled from their sheaths.

"What have you done with my friend?" Clemmy asked angrily.

"You are asking many questions when you should be making prayers."

And then blind rage overtook Clemmy. He turned to one side, reached out his arm and swept the grand vizier's table clean of food, silver goblets half full of wine and several maps on faded parchment paper. The dishes and silver clattered noisily to the ground. The interpreter dashed quickly to save the maps, which were splashed with wine. Clemmy felt the prick of a half dozen swords immediately. They were razor sharp, penetrated his woolen cloak and drew blood.

The surprised vizier leaped back and then shouted a command, which stopped the guards from finishing their killing strokes. Clemmy stood bent over, gasping for breath, stuck like a pin cushion, faint with pain.

Marbelard's Imperfect Prayer

Despite the pain of many wounds, Clemmy straightened himself and spoke again, softly this time.

"Where is my friend Magnus? Have you killed him for the glory of Allah?"

The grand vizier turned and shouted a command. After a moment, a group of the Sultan's guards appeared. In their midst was Magnus, still in his useless armor but bound with many ropes. He had been relieved of his sword and also of his boots. His eyes were fixed on the ground before him. His bare feet made large tracks in the dust.

It was, in fact, Magnus' feet that had given them away, for the Sultan had indeed tortured him. With a tail feather plucked from a parrot, Suleiman had tickled the big man's feet while a dozen guards had held him down.

Although Magnus felt miserable with humiliation and Clemmy was slumped in pain, when their eyes met, both men felt their spirits lift. They stood ten feet apart and were surrounded by Turkish blades. Knowing that their lives were forfeit brought a certain tenderness to the moment.

"You've spilled your juice," Magnus said, nodding at the table. Clemmy couldn't help smiling at his friend.

"You forgot your boots," he returned.

The morning sun at that moment emerged gloriously from behind the eastern foothills. A brilliant golden shaft made everything glow suddenly. It was a perfect sunrise on a day to remember. The door flap to the Sultan's tent was pulled aside and Suleiman the Magnificent strode into the morning air. His robes were of golden silk. In his white jeweled turban he looked to Clemmy like a snow-capped mountain peak. The curved blade of his sword flashed in the sunlight. All around them Magnus and Clemmy saw men drop to their knees and bow to the ground. Suleiman was helped onto a dancing black stallion, and then, taking the reins, he drew his sword and called out a loud command that brought the Turks back to their feet. He walked the fine horse toward Clemmy and Magnus.

Inside the palace, the yawning, peaceable King Fernholz was at that very moment hanging head and shoulders out of the royal bed, groping for his slippers.

On his perch at the top of the city wall, Marbelard stood behind his line of pilfered spoons. At that height the fully risen orange sun was reflected a dozen times in the polished silver.

And so it was war. Nearly thirty thousand Turk warriors, trained for mortal combat and willing to die for their Sultan, with sword, dagger and axe were set against one humpbacked village fool with twelve spoons.

In the stables below, Marbelard could hear hungry sheep bleating to be fed. He closed his eyes, and for the second time that day the air above Mulberia was swept by the wings of desperate but sincere, imperfect prayer.

"Dear God, it's me, Marbelard, keeper of the gates, praying for help. Can you hear me?"

The Sultan Suleiman, sitting proudly on his stallion, bestowed on Clemmy a conqueror's smile. He looked east into the sunrise for a moment and then spoke to the grand vizier. The interpreter echoed his words.

"Suleiman the Magnificent speaks of your courage, which he admires. He says that it is a good day to die."

Clemmy and Magnus looked sorrowfully at each other. Clemmy felt his own blood streaking down his thigh. He felt fear, guilt and many regrets overtaking him. He pictured in his mind the Lady Libby's lovely face and heard in his mind her wonderful laughter.

The Sultan spoke again and then spurred his

horse away, waving his sword over his head. A great clamor of war cries arose as Suleiman rode into the midst of his army and disappeared. The roar became deafening.

In his palace kitchen, King Fernholz, not yet awake enough to notice his perfect left leg, was puttering around, trying to make porridge. He had lit a fire and was grumbling about not being able to find a spoon.

On top of the city wall, Marbelard held one of the missing spoons aloft like a baton.

"If you can hear me, God, please help!" he shouted. His thoughts were interrupted suddenly by the roar of the Turks. He opened his eyes and saw to his terror that the enemy was galloping hard toward the city. He saw the swords waving and he could feel the earth trembling, even on his ledge.

"Dear God," he began again, groping for words. "Help!" he shouted, waving his spoon. "Turn our sheep into warhorses!" he blurted, forgetting that there was no one to ride them.

"Turn our spoons into swords!" he yelled into the sky. His wide-angle eyes filled with tears. The rest of his prayer consisted of yelling "HELP!" three times, long and loud. "HEEEEELLLP!"

And then he stopped his shouting. He sagged against the wall and stared dully at the screaming horde charging across the plain. And then, remembering himself, he said very softly, "Amen."

Ebb Tide

It was a day of sublime misproportion, of course: thousands against a few, warriors against cripples, a tide of war against an eddy of love. But in an instant the yowling Turks found themselves waving not their razor-sharp swords but spoons! Their saddles went slack and dropped; their horses shrank and became woolen, turned instantly into sheep! A great dusty pileup took place on the plain. Turks flew and bounced, head over heels, sash over turban. The roar of the charge was muffled into *oof*s and *aaowwgh*s and the bleating of thousands of squirming, terrified sheep. Back in his pantry King Fernholz thought for a moment, scratched his red beard and said, "A king with no sons is like a kitchen with no spoons."

It was true enough, if not exceptionally wise. The King without sons (or spoons) ate his porridge with a small wooden stirring stick.

With wide, unbelieving eyes, Marbelard saw the

Turks rolling somersaults on the sheep-shearing plain. The sheep that had been horses ran together into a great woolly flock, turning east toward the river. The dazed warriors dragged themselves to their feet and were milling about on the field in confusion.

Even bare-handed and on foot, of course, the Turks could still have conquered the city. But they had lost more than their blades and their horses. They had lost their will to fight. They assumed that they were beaten with magic! This idea spread among them. In panic they ran away, not unlike the sheep, only they went south in retreat, streaking past Suleiman, who sat on his rump staring with bewilderment at his spoon. The Turks themselves shouldered the heavy supply wagons and poured away on the road and into the forest.

Against the ebbing Moslem tide two figures made their way slowly. The larger, Magnus, stooped to support Clemmy, who hobbled and pressed his hand to his wounds. Magnus pushed his way through the mob, clearing a path with his strong right arm. More than once his bare feet were trod upon, but he suffered this bravely and pressed forward.

As they met and passed the foremost Turks (now rearmost), they found themselves suddenly alone. All about them were leather saddles and spoons. Spoons! Thousands of shining silver spoons were strewn across the field. Magnus and Clemmy stopped in wonder. They turned to see the enemy fleeing. Their backsides were disappearing in a cloud of dust.

"They've left their spoons," Magnus wondered aloud.

"Magnus . . ." Clemmy said quietly.

"And they have lost their horses." It was too much to take in. It was too strange to understand. Magnus gave up thinking and looked toward the city walls. He saw an unmistakable figure rushing, leaping toward them, bobbing his head and waving one arm.

"It's Marbelard," Magnus said. Taking hold of Clemmy again, he walked toward the city. The reflection of the sun in the jeweled Turk harnesses and in the spoons made flashing constellations on the ground all around them.

"Magnus," Clemmy said again.

"What?"

"I'm dying," he whispered. His legs gave way below him, and as darkness washed over him, he saw only the gleaming points of light, and then nothing at all.

Women

To his credit, King Fernholz of Mulberia wept at Clemmy's bedside. He reddened with shame when Magnus told him the whole story. His pleasure at being healed—unwarted, unfreckled and unlamed—became a source of guilt. He wept for himself as well as for his pale, bandaged and loyal friend. He had been correct, however, about God saving his kingdom from the Turk.

Moments after Magnus carried Clemmy into the palace, Aunt Lucia walked boldly in, demanding to know what was going on. She had heard the early-morning din as she had put on her teakettle. She had heard the drumming, howling and bleating, and was simply fed up with all the racket.

Finding Clemmy wounded, she immediately took over nursing duty and sent the men out of the room. Together, Lucia and Jude dressed Clemmy's wounds.

Wiping a tear, Jude said, "He's a good boy."

"Better than some," the matron allowed. It may have been the nicest thing she had ever said about a man.

Clemmy did not wake up, but he had no fever and he slept deeply. He was strong and he would heal. The women found Marbelard waiting outside the door, sick with worry. Jude took his withered hand with the silver ring.

"Clemmy is sleeping," she whispered and gave him a hopeful smile. "Marbelard."

"Yes?"

"You took my spoons."

"I . . . I borrowed them," he said.

"Well, go and get them. Quick!"

Marbelard straightened in surprise, and then he hurried away, weaving down the hallway and out the front door. You want spoons? I'll show you spoons!

In his garden King Fernholz found the deceased Shiefelbine sitting peacefully on his bench. Thinking him merely asleep, Fernholz sat beside him and tried to collect his thoughts.

"I've tried to be a good king," he said, eyeing the butterflies circling the old man's head.

"But a king must look to his heirs. He must marry and have sons." Shiefelbine's tattered marriage robe fluttered lightly in the breeze.

"It is my duty to the citizens of Mulberia," he

said, with a sweeping gesture of his arm that took in all his deserted kingdom.

In due course, the citizens began to return to the city. Among them came the merchant Chilton, brother to the matron Lucia and father of the Lady Libby. The shepherds rounded up the great new flock of sheep and divided them in the high pastures. The jeweled saddles and bridles were gathered by the weavers and cloth makers, and the spoons were stored in several large trunks inside Fernholz' palace (except for twelve that were unaccountably missing).

After a day or so of unchanging posture and at least two chats with the King, Shiefelbine was diagnosed to be not among the living. He was buried with dignity in the cemetery, along with his ratty old bag and the imperfect-prayer book, *En Supplico Mirabilis.*

In two weeks, under the watchful eyes of his two nurses, Clemmy was well enough to take a walk outside with King Fernholz. The King walked perfectly now and had a kingly appearance. He had not spoken of the lady since the dramatic events had left his friend infirm. Clemmy knew this was a strain for the King, and so he decided to broach the subject himself.

"Tomorrow," he said, "I will go see the Lady Libby and once more plead your case in marriage." The King was overjoyed.

And so he did, using a walking stick carved for

him by Magnus. He was accompanied by the matron, who introduced him to Libby's father, Master Chilton. The two men took tea in the sitting room. Through the high windows Clemmy saw Libby and Molina walking among the roses.

"I've brought a marriage proposal for your daughter, sir," Clemmy said.

"On whose behalf?"

"King Fernholz, sir."

Chilton drummed his fingers and drank from his teacup. The matron, of course, had told him everything that had happened while he was away.

"He's a good king," Clemmy said quickly. "He has overcome much to make himself worthy of her affections. At her request he has prayed for the removal of his wart and his freckles, and even of his stiff leg. And the prayers were heard! He has been healed of all these things."

Libby's father smiled at Clemmy and shook his head.

"She cares about none of these things," he said with a wave of his hand.

"But . . . she . . ."

"Women, you see, don't always say exactly what they mean. Surely you must have discovered this yourself."

Clemmy stared at the man. Master Chilton stood by the window. He watched the young women in the garden laughing at some joke of their own.

"I'll admit it's very irritating," Chilton said, "but there's no changing it. Women are funny creatures, my boy."

In the passageway the eavesdropping matron covered her mouth with her hands, nearly collapsing with laughter. Men are such idiots, she thought, as she took a deep breath and entered the sitting room.

"Clemmy," she said kindly, "will you do me a small favor?"

"Of course, anything." He rose from his chair and took hold of his walking stick.

"Will you please go into the garden and tell my daughter Molina to come here at once."

"I'll go!" Chilton offered.

Aunt Lucia turned and gave him a withering look. The man changed his mind immediately. The matron rolled her eyes with impatience and then turned again to Clemmy. She helped him to the door.

Moments later Molina, Master Chilton and Lucia all stood by the windows watching Clemmy and Libby across the yard. They saw Libby cut a perfect rose and offer it to Clemmy.

"Do you love me, Clemmy?" Libby asked, blushing slightly but holding his gaze.

"More than my life," he answered. They surrendered everything and promised everything to each other with the look that passed between them. And then Clemmy kissed the red rose and touched it to her cheek.

The Wind

"I want to marry the Lady Libby," Clemmy said bluntly to the King when he had returned to the palace, still holding the precious flower. To his surprise, Fernholz accepted the news with dignity. He clasped both his hands on Clemmy's shoulders, looked him square in the eye and said, "I approve!"

"I'm sure you must be disappointed, but—"

"Don't say another word," the King interrupted him. "I've changed my mind!" he said emphatically. Clemmy was amazed.

The truth of the matter was that while Clemmy was away, Jude had spoken with Fernholz about the young lovers. It was a conspiracy of sorts between her and Aunt Lucia. The King was at first stunned, then hurt, then grievously disappointed.

"Don't be a silly king," Jude said affectionately. Fernholz wiped a tear.

"And besides," she told him, "come closer and I'll tell you a secret."

She whispered in his ear the name of Molina, and she arched her old eyebrows and lifted her red cheeks with a grin.

"The cabbage thrower?" Fernholz wondered aloud.

"Mmmmm," Jude said with a nod.

In the weeks that followed, Marbelard helped Clemmy adjust to walking with the King's limp.

"Like this!" Marbelard laughed, and bobbed ahead. Marbelard was made the new official doorman by King Fernholz. Whenever Clemmy returned from his walks to visit Magnus in the sheep pastures outside the city walls, Marbelard would hurry out to meet him. Together, limping and shuffling along happily, they passed through the great doors of the city.

Magnus shed his helmet and breastplate for good. He vowed to do no more soldiering and went back to being a simple (and very large) shepherd. It was Magnus who convinced Clemmy and Jude that they should make the city of Mulberia their new home.

"It's a fine place to live, usually," Magnus said, and frightened away an entire flock of sheep with his loud laughter.

The Lady Libby and Clemmy, sitting together on the King's bench, talked shyly of marriage one day. "What about my wart?" Clemmy asked, remembering her very own words spoken only weeks before.

"It's just a little wart," she answered.

"And my freckles?"

"Some men look better with a few freckles," she said.

"Well, what about my limp?" Clemmy asked, just to make sure.

"You have a limp?" she teased him. "Then you will never be able to run away from me!"

Though there were no Turks in attendance, there was a royal wedding in Mulberia when the summer turned into autumn. Fernholz, being a truly wise king, had turned his attentions toward the doting Molina even before Clemmy's red rose dropped its petals.

King Fernholz' wedding was a happy and grand occasion, attended by all the citizens and presided over by none other than Brother Hans, who sang out his fine Latin phrases for all to hear. When the danger of the Turk had passed, the starving monks had found their way back to the monastery, where they gave thanks to God for Hans' wonderful turnips. Even the wandering merchant Balfounder found his way to Mulberia in time to make a handsome profit selling wedding presents.

Weaving slightly in the front row,
Marbelard closed his eyes and prayed
earnestly that King Fernholz and his
Queen would bear many children.
Above the heads of
everyone the west
wind swirled.

*The
End*